Generations

By Frank G. Davis

GENERATIONS

3

GENERATIONS

4

Copyright © 2020
Frank G. Davis

ISBN # 978-1-954253-50-6

9 8 7 6 5 4 3 2 1

Editing, Cover, & Layout by: solfire@phoenix-farm.com

Dedication

This book is dedicated to three of my best friends. Each one of them inspired me in different, but very significant ways. All three of them have passed away. I miss them every day.

Sergeant David Lawrence, USMC, Recon—Dave had one tour in Vietnam and had some of the most terrifying war stories I have ever heard. The war changed him in so many ways, none of them good. We were power-lifting training partners for many years. He was rated an Elite Class lifter and was on the top one hundred list for the dead lift every year he competed. He had a quirky sense of humor and liked to share jokes. He made me laugh.

Sergeant Henry White, USAF—Henry was also one of my training partners in power lifting. He was the strongest of us. He held Arizona state records in the bench press and squat for several years and was also an Elite Class lifter. He was rated in the top five in the United States for five years in a row. At his funeral, one of his other friends described Henry as "A party waiting to happen." It described Henry perfectly. I used that phrase in the book to describe the Commander White character.

Doctor John Sanborn, PhD—John was one of the smartest men I've known. I worked with him for many years as aerospace engineers. He eventually became my boss and leader of our gas turbine, design and development group. He introduced us to computer modeling and was largely responsible for updating our design methods. More importantly to me, he was a great friend. Tragically, he passed away from ALS at the peak of his career.

GENERATIONS

6

Part 1

The Heretic

GENERATIONS

8

Protector Kaplan

I was the first one to see him. Protector Graves and I were having lunch at an outdoor café just inside Gate 3N. Graves was bored and I was scanning the passing crowd in the plaza as I ate.

"Come here little fly," said Graves. "Look what I have for you. It's your favorite food, all sweet and sugary, *yum yum*." A fly on the table was making a random walking pattern that took it close to Grave's wand. When it sensed the drop of syrup, the fly scurried quickly to the wand and began to feed. "Will you look at that!" exclaimed Graves. "I've got the wand set on three and it has no effect."

"Quit torturing the bugs, Graves," I said as I pushed the last of my meat roll into my mouth while continuing to watch the crowd.

"That's just the point," he responded. "I'm not torturing them; they don't feel a thing. Let's see what level eight does."

I quickly glanced at Graves to be sure no one was standing close to him. "Be careful with the wand," I warned.

"Relax, Kaplan. You worry too much. And quit staring at the crowd, you're making people nervous. This is Ring 3, not the Outer Ring; nothing ever happens here."

Graves shook off the feeding fly and tapped the wand control to a level eight setting. The fly began circling, moving closer to the wand. My scanner went off.

"What've you got?" asked Graves.

"Citizen without his star," I answered, not looking up as I checked the scanner display. "I'll take it. You play with your bugs." As I got up and stared to move through the crowd, I heard a *zap* behind me followed by a giggle from Graves.

10

The lunchtime crowd was pretty heavy, but as usual, it parted as I moved in the direction of the sinner; no one wanted to get in the way of a protector. There was no mistaking him. I could tell by his clothes that he wasn't one of the chosen; he was wearing a light blue, one-piece jumpsuit with a tight fitting hood covering most of his head and neck. Almost all of the chosen wear loose fitting white robes; none of them wear jumpsuits. My first reaction was to wonder how he had gotten into Ring 3. The protectors at Gate 3N were going to have to be disciplined.

He was standing by himself, looking up at the buildings on either side of the plaza, slowly turning to take it all in, a look of curiosity on his face. His face … if I had any doubts before … one look at his face was all I needed to tell me he was not one of the chosen. His skin was dark with a yellow cast, wisps of short, jet black hair peeked out from under his hood, but it was his eyes … it was his eyes that stopped me in my tracks. They were a dark walnut shade of *brown.*

I touched my communicator, "Graves, I need backup, now."

The sinner turned at the sound of my voice and smiled at me showing perfect white teeth. "Good day to you, citizen," I said in as calm a voice as I could manage. "You seem to have forgotten your star." He looked puzzled and started to speak just as Graves came up slightly behind him.

"Yes, citizen," said Graves, "the Star of David, your ID star. The one they gave you when you came in through the Outer Gate. From the looks of your clothes that couldn't have been too long ago."

He started to turn toward Graves, but turned back as I asked, "What are you doing in Ring 3? Don't you remember what

Orientation explained to you about staying in the Outer Ring until you are chosen?"

"I didn't come through the Outer Gate," he said in a heavily accented voice.

"Of course, you did. Every Gentile comes through the Outer Gate. You must have forgotten," said Graves sarcastically.

The sinner started to turn again, but Graves had moved to the other side, still behind him, with his wand in his hand. Like a yo-yo he turned back as I said, "You have sinned, citizen, and as Protectors of the Law it is our job to punish sinners. Going without your star is a level one sin. After you are punished, we will find out how you got into Ring 3; there will probably be additional punishment required."

He took a step back and put out both hands in front of him to ward me off as I moved forward. "Now wait a minute. You can't punish me … I'm not one of you … I'm not from here …"

Graves stepped forward and laid the wand on his shoulder.

There should have been a slight zap, a simple shock, to serve as a reminder that everyone has to obey the law or suffer the consequences. Instead, there was a blinding flash and a clap of thunder as Graves and the stranger were ripped apart. Graves must have flown ten yards through the air before landing hard on a peddler's cart. His wand dropped straight down with a clattering sound practically at my feet. The stranger looked like a fireworks display. Blue-white sparks danced over his body as he lay jerking and twitching on the ground five yards away. Smoke was rising from the body as I stood there in shock.

A small crowd of curious citizens had gathered while Graves and I interrogated the stranger. There is always an element of the population who enjoys watching others get punished. But no one could have anticipated what just happened. Most scattered before the bodies hit the plaza tile. Only a few remained to gawk. A young woman came running up. Her eyes grew wide at the sight of the smoldering stranger. "Someone help him!" she cried. And then, when no one moved, she snatched a cape off the man standing next to her and flung it over the stranger's body and began to pat out the sparks.

"Hey, you stole my cape! Stop that. You're going to ruin it. Protector, stop that woman! She stole my cape!"

He grabbed my arm and tried to pull me toward the woman who was furiously trying to put out the fire. His touch startled me out of my shock. At the same moment, he realized his error; nobody ever touches a protector.

"Protector, please forgive me," he pleaded as he backed away shaking his hands as if to get the touch of me off of his skin. "But she stole my cape," he ended in a fearful whimper.

I moved to the woman and grabbed her by the arms lifting her away from the stranger. I flung the cape in the direction of the still protesting man. "If you have a complaint, file it with the judge." I glared at him and he backed quickly away inspecting his smoking cape.

"It's ruined," he whined, "That woman ruined my new cape. She's going to have to pay. And I want her punished too. She stole it."

I hardly heard him. I was looking at the stranger's body. The fire was out, but there was a strong smell of burnt flesh. I rolled him over and checked for a pulse; it was weak, but he was still alive. I touched my communicator. "This is Protector Kaplan. I have a medical emergency. I have a citizen and a protector down. Burns and electrical shock. Plaza near Gate 3N."

There was brief static in my left ear plug before the reply. "We copy, protector. Med team will be there in two minutes."

"Better send a security priest too," I added.

There was a pause. "Nature of the sin?"

"Citizen has no star and has … unusual physical appearance. Probable security violation."

"Copy. Security Priest Simon will arrive shortly. You are not to leave the scene until dismissed by SP Simon."

"Understood. Out."

Graves was slowly walking toward me on shaky legs.

"You okay?"

He shook his head. "I don't think so … hurt all over. What happened?"

I walked back to what remained of his wand and picked it up. It was badly damaged; one end had partially melted and the black plasteel was twisted out of shape. I looked at the control setting and shook my head. I handed the wand back to Graves and I heard the quick gasp as he saw the setting. It was still on level eight.

We stood silently waiting for the security priest to arrive.

Security Priest Simon

The med team was already treating the injured when I arrived on the scene. One man was lying on the ground and his clothes were smoking. The techs were placing him on a power gurney. There were two protectors standing nearby and another tech was checking one of them over. "Protector Kaplan?"

14

"I'm Kaplan," said the second protector. He was tall, good looking, with wavy blonde hair and blue eyes. He was also very young.

"I'm Security Priest Simon. You called in a probable security violation?"

He nodded and gestured towards the man on the ground. "This citizen didn't have his star and I don't think he is chosen."

"You mentioned something about his appearance being strange?" The protector looked down at his feet and mumbled something I couldn't quite hear. "Speak up, man," I snapped.

His head came up quickly. "Sorry, SP. I said that his eyes had a funny shape and they … they were brown."

"Brown?" I snorted and shook my head. "How long have you been a protector?"

"Almost three years, SP," he answered quickly.

"And during those 'almost three years,' how many brown eyed people have you seen?"

"This was my first one."

"I don't believe it for a minute." The med techs had started driving the gurney towards the hospital. "Tech, please bring that citizen here. He has not been released," I said in an annoyed tone.

"SP, the man may die if he doesn't get immediate attention," answered one of the techs.

"The Law will be served," I said quietly. "Bring him here."

Without further argument, they drove the gurney next to Protector Kaplan and me. The man did have oddly shaped eyes, but it was hard to tell if they were naturally that way or had been affected by the wand discharging. I placed my thumb on his right eyelid and peeled it back. The eye was brown. I looked closely; there was no colored contact over the iris, it was truly brown.

Astonishing! "It looks like I owe you an apology, Protector." I took my scanner out of its holder. "Computer, retina scan for ID."

The computer's electronic voice responded, "Proceed."

I waved the scanner over the stranger's eye until I heard the beep and then stepped back. Two seconds later the computer said, "Subject cannot be identified. Retina pattern is not on file."

I stood there lost in thought until one of the techs coughed lightly to get my attention. "Oh, yes. I'm through with the citizen. Take him to the hospital." As they drove off, I added. "Keep him alive. He has lots of questions to answer." I turned back to the protector. "Now, I want you to tell me exactly what happened."

Senior Healer Johnson

"We have a bad one, Madam Healer." The med tech was driving the gurney into the OR. I could see smoke rising from the patient's head and shoulders.

"What happened?" asked my apprentice.

"A protector hit him with a level eight."

"Level eight! Good Lord, what did he do, kill someone?"

The techs lifted the man from the gurney to the operating table. "Naw, he just showed up in Ring 3 without his star." They placed him on the treatment bed and stretched him out. "I think it was an accident; it should have been only a level one sin. Well he's all yours now," said a tech as they stared to leave. "Oh, by the way. A security priest said you need to keep him alive. He has to answer lots of questions."

"Wonderful," I said sarcastically. "Well, Junior, are you ready to go to work?"

16

"Thirty more seconds in the sterilization field, Senior Healer," he answered.

I pulled my hands out of the field and walked over to the table. "Computer, vital signs."

The electronic voice answered immediately, "Pulse weak and erratic, pressure sixty over thirty and falling, respiration … five to eight." There was barely a perceptible pause before it continued, "Unusual brain wave patterns, possible memory blank. Second and third degree burns over seventy-five percent of his body. Prognosis is extremely poor."

"Says you," I said under my breath.

Junior hurried to the table giving the computer instructions as he and I looked at the patient. "Stabilize the vital signs and notify us if anything gets worse."

"Working," the computer answered.

"Let's get his clothes off of him and see how bad the burns really are."

Junior looked up at me in surprise, "Don't you believe the computer's appraisal?"

"I like to see things for myself." I took the laser scalpel and sliced down the front of his jumpsuit, only it didn't slice. It didn't leave a mark or even seem to get hot, although it was hard to be certain. I tried again on a higher setting with the same results. "Strange, we know it burns. Why won't the laser cut it?"

"Try a blade," suggested Junior.

I did but the suit still wouldn't cut. Junior was looking at the suit now, checking it over to see how we could get it off. In the process, he touched a stud on the collar and a seam that I would have sworn wasn't there a second ago parted from the neck to the crotch and curled back. It revealed a dark-skinned torso, relatively

17

free from body hair, covered with a fine square pattern of burn lines spaced about a quarter inch apart. At the shoulder, apparently where the protector's wand had touched him, there was a two inch hole in the suit. The ends of small diameter wires could be seen at the edge of the hole, apparently woven into the cloth. When the suit opened up it seemed to get loose all over and the hood fell back from his head. His hair was singed and it had the unmistakable odor of burnt hair, but it was the color that caused me to do a double take. It was jet black, very unusual. And then I noticed the shape of his eyes and a chill ran up my spine. I recognized the epicanthic folds from some very old data banks I had scanned in medical history class. Somewhat hesitantly, I placed my thumb on the eye lid and pushed it open.

Junior gasped, "My God, his eyes are brown. How can that be?"

"I don't know, but I bet we're going to have to find out, and soon too. No wonder the security priest wants to ask him some questions."

Junior and I quickly got him out of his jumpsuit and into the burn tank, hooked up IVs and monitor leads, and set parameter flags for the computer.

"What now?" asked Junior.

"I want a data dump to my computer on his blood work as soon as possible," I said as I walked to my office. "And I want someone with him full time."

"You mean a nurse?"

"A nurse, an orderly, an aide; I don't care. I just don't want him alone for a minute. They are to call me the first time he shows any sign of conciousness. You got that? I'll sleep in my office until this is over," I said as I rubbed my eyes. I could feel a tension headache coming on.

18

"Is he that important?"

"Son, this man is going to be the most important thing to happen in New Jerusalem since Moses founded the city."

Junior blanched, turned, and hurried off to find someone to baby-sit the stranger. I walked into my office and poured a glass of water. I held the glass to my forehead and felt the coolness help ease the tension. I walked to the monitor and sat down with a thump and slowly sipped the water. I took a deep breath, let it out slowly.

"Well," I said to myself, "you'd better get to work. Computer, access all files on The Plague."

Servant Anna

I was cleaning my master's quarters when Junior Healer Murphy came running into the room. He was out of breath and had a strange, almost wild look on his face. "Anna!" he said in an excited voice, "you're perfect. Come with me."

Perfect? I'd been called many things in my young life but I don't recall anyone saying I was perfect. In fact, I don't recall ever hearing any indentured servant called perfect. Junior grabbed me by the wrist and was almost dragging me down the hall towards the hospital. "Wait," I protested. "I'm not allowed in the hospital area. Senior Healer Johnson will be every upset…"

"It's alright, Anna. I'm following Senior Healer's orders. You have a new job now. We'll get someone else to do the cleaning."

That was the best news I'd heard in over a year. I stopped resisting and began to run faster. "What is this new job?" I asked as we passed through the hospital doors.

19

"We have a new patient. A very important patient and he needs to be watched constantly."

We walked into a recovery room. In the center was a large tank. There was a body in it but I couldn't see much because it was completely covered in a blue-green liquid. "What am I supposed to do?"

"You will stay with the patient until relieved. A bed will be brought in for you and you will take your meals here. If he makes any movements you are to call either myself or Senior Healer Johnson immediately." Junior turned and left abruptly. I walked over to the tank and looked in then stepped quickly back, my heart pounding in my chest. He was completely naked. I had never seen a naked man before. It was quite … different.

The novelty of this new work wore off quickly. After a few days I became bored. Even looking at the patient's … difference became boring. Junior would come in from time to time to make sure all the tubes attached to the patient were firmly in place. He would make adjustments to the nutrient mix and medications and then leave. I almost never saw Senior Healer anymore. When I asked Junior about her, he said she had locked herself in her office and was studying the computer database.

On the fourth day, a security priest arrived. At first, I thought he had come for me and my heart skipped a beat as I tried to remember if I had committed any sin. But he ignored me and walked directly to the tank and looked at the patient. Then quickly, he turned to me and said, "Stop singing. It's very annoying."

I closed my mouth quickly. I hadn't realized I had been singing. I always sing when I'm alone to pass the time. And I'm almost always alone. I had forgotten to stop when the SP entered. "Sorry, Your Holiness. It won't happen again."

20

He glared at me with cold piercing eyes. "I'm not your Holiness. I am Security Priest Simon or SP. Only the Moses or our Lord are to be addressed as Your Holiness. The next time you address me incorrectly, I will use my wand to refresh your memory."

I nodded and backed away not daring to speak again. The thought of the wand terrified me. Just then Senior Healer came in; she must have heard the SP on the monitors. "Good day to you, Security Priest Simon. How may we be of assistance?"

"How soon?" he asked. It sounded like a question he had asked several times before.

Senior Healer sighed and moved forward to look at the monitors. "He's making excellent progress. This type of injury would have killed most men. He should be out of the burn tank by the end of the week. But he will remain unconscious for several more days, perhaps weeks."

The SP slammed his hands down on the side of the burn tank and turned on the Senior Healer. "I don't have weeks. I may not have days or even an hour." He thrust his finger at the floating body in the tank. "He could be a spy for an army of people like himself, an advanced scout checking on our defenses. He got into Ring 3 before he was detected and I must know how he did that." He stopped shouting and continued in a quieter voice that was even more terrifying. "You will use whatever medical skills you may have, or prayer, or magic, or any witchcraft that you may know, and you will make this man capable of talking to me within three days." He thrust three fingers in front of Senior Healer's face. "Do you understand me? Three days, no more. I will be back the day after Sabbath and he better be able to talk."

He pushed passed Senior Healer and stormed out of the room. Senior Healer let out a sigh and her shoulders sagged. She slowly turned and left the room.

I was alone with the patient. I began singing again. It was a sad song.

The Stranger

My first memories were of the sound of a young girl singing. Her voice was sweet and clear but the accent was so heavy that I could barely understand the words. I would drift from sleep to being nearly conscious and her voice would almost always be there. It gave me a feeling of well-being, which was strange because I knew I was in bad shape. I couldn't move and I couldn't see. All I could do was hear her songs but somehow that comforted me. I figured out I must have gotten hurt, that I was in a hospital, but I was so doped up I couldn't think clearly. All I could do was listen to her songs.

Then one morning I woke up and I couldn't hear the songs any longer. All I could hear was the sound of someone screaming, screaming as if they were in unbearable pain. I kept wanting the screaming to stop, the pain to go away. I wanted the songs again, but I couldn't stop screaming. Wait a minute. *It's me screaming!*

I opened my eyes but at the time I didn't know what I was seeing. Later, many hours later, when they found just the right mix of drugs that would reduce the pain to manageable levels and still allow me to be awake, I remembered what I had seen. It was like I was watching it all from a corner of the ceiling. I could see this person lying on the bed with his head bandaged, his arms and legs

22

restrained, screaming his lungs out. A young woman in her late teens or early twenties was cowering in the corner, terrified of the screams and the pain they indicated. Standing over me was a heavy-set, older woman holding a syringe gun trying to give me a sedative. A short, nasty looking man was restraining her.

"I must question him. I must do it now. Don't put him back to sleep yet. Don't you realize how important it is that I question him?" He kept saying words to this effect.

But the woman answered back, "He's going into shock. If you don't let me sedate him, he will die and then you will never get your answers."

It was like looking at an old-time picture, no movement, little color, everything in black and white and shades of gray.

Once they got the mix right, the nasty little guy was back almost immediately. "Who are you and what are you doing in New Jerusalem? And don't try to lie. I'll know if you're lying."

Panic started to rise in me. I felt a cold chill go down my spine causing me to involuntarily shiver. In a shaky voice, weak from lack of use, I said, "I don't know. I don't know who I am. I can't … can't remember my name." I felt tears start to run down my cheeks and I tried to wipe them away, but I was still restrained.

Nasty said, "Computer, verify." His voice was flat and unemotional as he looked at me with his cold, pale blue eyes.

"The subject is telling the truth."

"Damn!" Nasty said as he slammed his fist on the side of my bed.

Stocky Lady said to him, "I told you there was a good chance he had a memory blank. High wand settings sometimes do that."

Nasty waved his hand dismissing her comments. "When will he have his memory back? How long must I wait?"

23

Stocky Lady answered, "There's no way to predict. In some cases, it can last a few days; in others it lasts the rest of their life."

"That's unacceptable. Make it happen sooner. I don't care what you have to do to him, but make it happen soon, very soon." Nasty turned and left abruptly.

Stocky Lady turned to a younger man whom I assumed was her assistant. "We need to talk, Anna. You stay with the patient, talk to him."

"What should I talk about?" asked Anna.

"Tell him about yourself, how you got here, it doesn't matter, just get his mind working again. If his memory is going to come back, it will come back in bits and pieces. It seldom comes all at once. Ask him questions from time to time. See if he remembers anything, anything at all. Let me know as soon as he starts remembering." With that, Stocky Lady and Assistant Boy left the room leaving me alone with the girl.

Thinking back on that discussion made me feel like I was invisible. They talked like I wasn't even in the room or too stupid to understand. There was no concern for my feelings beyond how it affected getting information out of me. Nobody asked how I felt. Did it bother me that I didn't even know my own name? Or where I came from? Or why Nasty hated me so much? Or even what I looked like? Yes, all those things bothered me; they bothered me very much, thank you.

Anna was starring at me, her blue eyes wide with … I don't know what … excitement maybe. The top of my head was bandaged and I had some kind of dark glasses or goggles covering my eyes. She moved closer to my bed and double checked to make sure my restraints were in place. "You must have committed a very great sin to have upset the security priest so much."

24

I eased back; hurt all over and I felt weak and very, very tired. "I don't remember committing any sin. I really don't remember anything."

She moved closer, leaning over me, trying to look through the goggles into my eyes. I could smell the freshness of her hair, for some reason it reminded me of her voice when she sang. "Thank you for singing to me. You have a very pleasant voice."

She stood up straight and moved back a step. "You heard me singing?" she asked, a hint of fear in her voice. "Please don't tell Security Priest Simon. He told me to stop, that it was annoying. If he finds out I disobeyed him, he will punish me."

"I didn't find it annoying. It was comforting."

"That doesn't matter, the SP gave me instructions and I disobeyed him. If he finds out he'll use the wand on me."

"The wand?"

"Yes, of course, the wand, the 'instrument of correction' used to punish us when we sin. That's how you got here. A protector touched you with a wand. It was supposed to be a punishment for a minor sin. But the protector made a mistake; the pain setting was too high and it … it hurt you so badly you had to be brought to the hospital. Don't you remember anything?"

"No, Anna, nothing."

There was a long pause and then she said, "What would you like me to talk about?"

"I don't know … tell me about the city, tell me about yourself, tell me how you got here. No, wait. Tell me about myself, everything you know about me."

She laughed softly. "That's not very much."

"Anything will help," I pleaded.

"Well," she began, "you're a man, a Gentile. But you're different than any man I've ever met."

"Different? How am I different?"

"Lots of ways … your skin is kind of … an unusual color. So is your hair. And Junior said your eyes are brown, but I must have misunderstood."

"Why do you say that?"

She looked a little bit incredulous and then she shrugged her shoulders. "Because there haven't been any brown-eyed people on Earth since The Plague. You don't remember about The Plague either?"

I shook my head. "No, tell me about it."

"Well, I've only been in New Jerusalem for a few years. I've been indentured to the Senior Healer most of that time so I haven't had a lot of schooling, but even before I came to New Jerusalem I knew about The Plague. Even the Gentiles know about that."

"Sorry. Maybe it will come to me if you tell me something about it."

She sighed it was a sad sound. "About two hundred years ago there was this terrible disease we now just call The Plague. It killed off almost all of Earth's population, only blue-eyed people survived. It took less than ten years before The Plague ran its course, but by then there wasn't much left. The time after The Plague, before the Moses founded New Jerusalem, is called the Time of Chaos, some people call it the Time of Riots. People acted like animals: civilization just … just died." She paused and looked expectantly at me, but I just shook my head. She continued, "No one knows what caused The Plague but the ancients, even with all their advanced science, couldn't find a cure."

"Why did it kill only people with brown eyes?"

She shrugged again. "I don't know. Maybe it killed some blue-eyed people too. But it killed all the ones with brown eyes. I'm sure of that."

She stopped talking and began slowly walking around the room, running her finger over surfaces as if she were checking for dust. Finally, she ended up at the chair at the side of my bed and sat down. She was staring at me, at my dark glasses, staring intently. Finally, she had to ask. "What color are they? Are they brown?"

"I don't know Anna; I really don't. I don't even know what I look like."

She looked disappointed, but then a hint of a smile touched her face. "Would you like to find out?" she said almost in a whisper. "I could get a mirror."

I'm not sure why, but I hesitated, what if they're brown? What would that mean? Who knows? But I decided that wasn't what was bothering me. What if I didn't recognize myself? What if I saw a stranger looking back? How would that make me feel?

"Well?" said Anna with growing excitement.

"Sure," I said with feigned nonchalance. "Get a mirror."

Anna jumped out of the chair and was gone before I finished the sentence. She was back immediately with a large hand mirror. She held the mirror in front of my face and carefully lifted off my dark glasses.

"Oh my!"

I wasn't sure who said that. Maybe it was both of us. Because we were both stunned. I would have sworn I'd never seen the person in the mirror before; never seen anyone remotely like him. My eyes were brown; no mistaking that, but there was more. The shape of my eyes was different, not as round as the people I had seen, they looked slanted and half closed. I turned and looked at Ann and saw … I'm not sure what.

"Anna, are you Ok?"

She tried to speak, but nothing came out. Finally she nodded her head, slowly at first, but then faster until she looked like some kind of broken jack-in-the-box. Then she stopped abruptly and looked down at her lap.

"Are you sure you're all right?"

Her head came up slowly, but she looked straight at me as she said in her musical voice, "You're the most beautiful man I've ever seen."

Junior Healer Murphy

I followed Senior Healer out of the patent's room into her office. She was visibly upset. I tried to offer some words of encouragement. "SP Simon is being unreasonable. He's under a lot of pressure himself, but I'm sure he must realize there's a limit to what we can do."

She sat down heavily in her chair and turned to look at me and shook her head. She gestured to the couch and I sat down. "I'm afraid you don't know the SP like I do. He doesn't care if his request is impossible. He'll expect that we do the impossible or suffer the consequences. We need to do everything we can to help our patient get his memory back." She drummed her fingers on her desk and seemed lost in thought for a moment. I sat respectfully quiet and let her contemplate the path the treatment should take. After a few minutes, she looked at me and said. "Junior, I'm going to do a database search on treatment for memory blanks to be sure I haven't overlooked anything. I want you to implement the treatment we've outlined so far. You are to see him everyday and question him about his past. Spend at least a half hour with him each morning and again each afternoon."

"Should I have Anna go back to her housekeeping duties?" I asked.

Senior healer shook her head. "No, I want Anna to stay with him. Encourage her to be friendly, have her talk with him and help him with some physical therapy."

"But Senior Healer, Anna's only an indentured servant. She doesn't know anything about physical therapy."

"Well show her, for heaven's sake. It's not like he's had some serious physical injury, he just needs to get back his strength and flexibility. It will give her an excuse to stay with him and talk, not that she needs much of excuse."

I must have looked puzzled because Senior Healer smiled and said, "Junior, haven't you been paying attention? Haven't you seen the way she looks at him?"

I sat up straight, somewhat embarrassed by the direction the conversation was heading. "No, I can't say I have."

"Well trust me, Anna will be delighted to stay, and she may well be the best thing we have to help restore his memory."

The Stranger

During my stay in the hospital, Anna was always with me. She was there in the morning when I woke up, and in the evening when I went to sleep. Nasty came in at least twice a day, always his cheerful, happy-go-lucky self. Always the same question. Always the same answer. Stocky Lady, aka Senior Healer Johnson, and her faithful companion, aka Junior, would come in every day and poke, probe, and shoot stuff into my veins. They would ask me all kinds of questions about my earliest memories. I would continue to answer just as I had when I woke up in the hospital, screaming my brains out. No one ever said, "How do you feel today, better?" In fact, with the exception of Anna, I got the distinct impression everyone else would just as soon never see me again.

Physical therapy had begun the day I was conscious. They put muscle stimulators on me when I got out of the burn tank. Anna was instructed on how to move my limbs through a full range of motion to help maintain some level of flexibility while I was comatose. But it was still a major pain to start using muscles that hadn't seen any real activity for several weeks. While Anna helped me through the exercise routines, we talked.

"How did you know I wasn't one of the Chosen?" I asked between deep knee bends.

"Well, that was pretty obvious. You don't have the mark of Abraham."

"Oh," I managed to grunt out as I straightened up. "Was that the ninth squat or tenth?"

"Eighth. Two more."

"What's the mark of Abraham?" I asked, as I started down on the ninth.

She hesitated and looked a little embarrassed, then said in a shy voice, "You haven't been circumcised."

"Oh," I grunted out again. "That's nine." *Puff, puff* … "What's it mean to be circumcised?"

30

That question seemed too much for her to bear and she turned away but not before I caught a glimpse of the deep scarlet flush on her cheek. With her back turned she said, "They cut off the end of your … your manhood."

I had started down for number ten and had reached the bottom as she hit me with that news. I felt, or imagined I felt, a sharp pain in my groin and toppled over backwards. I had to overcome the urge to grab myself.

Anna was there in a flash, helping me up. "Are you alright?" she asked, truly concerned for my well-being,

"Yes," I stammered. "I'm fine. Just a little shocked by your answer." I turned and looked at her face to see if I could detect any indication she might be teasing me, but she seemed serious. "Could I sit down for a moment please?" I asked and sat down heavily on the closest chair.

"It's really not so bad. Everyone of the men in New Jerusalem has it done before they become Chosen."

"How much do they cut off?"

"Just a little bit of the end. It's all skin."

"What do women have to cut off to be Chosen?"

"Nothing. Only the men have the mark of Abraham."

"That doesn't seem fair. Women should have to suffer too."

"Well, I'm glad they don't."

I stood back up and started doing toe touches when something occurred to me. "How did you know I wasn't circumcised?"

The crimson returned to her cheeks. "Well, I had to wash you, didn't I? Senior Healer said I should wash you all over everyday or you could get sick."

I looked at her and I couldn't help smiling at her mild discomfort. "So," I said as I looked at my toes and reached down to touch the floor, "How many other men have you … washed?" I snuck a quick peak at her as I held the stretch, placing both palms on the floor.

She was smiling now. "You're the first one." There was a hint of excitement in her voice.

By the end of a couple weeks of therapy, I felt pretty good. Although I had no way of knowing for sure, I felt almost back to one hundred percent of my old self, at least physically. My memory still eluded me so most of the conversations with Anna had been one sided. Her descriptions of New Jerusalem and its history were particularly interesting.

About two hundred years after The Plague, the Moses founded New Jerusalem. Senior Healer says the Lord led him to this spot. It's a place of the ancients. He was all alone and was trying to avoid the scavenging gangs in this area when he fell into a pit. It turns out that pit was an opening into an ancient laboratory.

"Tell me about the Moses. Was that his name or some kind of title?"

"No one knows the real name of the first Moses, well actually he wasn't the first. The first was from the Book."

"The book?"

"The Holy Book, the one the Moses used to learn to read." She walked around the room as I exercised, checking to make sure I was doing the drills correctly. "Senior Healer says the Moses' father taught him to read using the remains of a very old book. During the Time of Chaos, there was hardly anyone left who could read. But the father of the Moses told him that his father taught him to read and made him promise to teach his children to read. He said that when the Time of Chaos ended the world was going to need educated people to help rebuild. They all used the Book.

It was passed down from generation to generation since the days of The Plague. It's not really a whole book, only part of one."

"What's the book about?"

"It's a story about the beginning of time, of how our Lord selected a group of people to be the Chosen. It tells how the Chosen have to have the mark of Abraham as a sign to the world that they are God's people."

I hesitated in the middle of a pushup as she mentioned the mark of Abraham again. I wonder if I had what it takes to become Chosen. Actually, I was wondering if I was willing to sacrifice a portion of my private parts to stay with Anna. I didn't answer that. "What else does the book say?"

"It tells about how the Lord's Chosen people were made slaves and how a great leader named Moses took them out of slavery to the Promised Land. That's where they built the city of Jerusalem."

I struggled through the fiftieth pushup then sat back on my heels and felt the burn on my chest, shoulder, and arms. It was a good feeling, a familiar feeling. I massaged the back of my arms and thought about what Anna said. Something about the story seemed familiar.

"Anna, why did this guy in the pit think he was the new Moses?"

"He had a vision. The Lord came to him and said he was to be the new Moses; the new leader of a new nation. The Book had told about the laws the Lord gave to the original Moses. If they obeyed the laws, the Lord would protect them and make them a strong nation and nothing could hurt them, but if they did not follow His laws, He would turn his back on them. In the vision, the new Moses saw the reason for The Plague. The world was being punished for not following the laws. Now it was time to set up a

New Jerusalem, based on the old laws. In the vision, the Lord made the same promise to the new Moses as he made to the old one; follow my laws and I will make you a strong nation."

Junior Healer Murphy

It seems Senior Healer was right. During the next few days, as the stranger's strength returned, Anna was constantly by his side. I taught her a few basic exercises to strengthen the large muscle groups and some flexibility movements. She attacked the assignment with a passion. Every time I would come into the recovery room, she had him doing exercises, either stretching or situps, or pushups, or something else equally as strenuous. I had thoughts to caution her about doing too much too soon, but the patient seemed to thrive on the activity. And there was something more. It was the way Anna looked at him, the way she was always by his side as close as she dared when she wasn't touching him. And she touched him as much as she dared, helping him with his exercises. I got the impression that Anna was having him work out so often to give her an excuse to touch him.

Even though the patient responded well to the physical therapy, we made little progress in helping him to regain his memory. Twice a day, as Senior Healer instructed, I would visit him. During the course of my examinations and treatments, we would talk, but any memory prior to his waking up in the hospital seemed to be non-existent. So most of the time he would ask me questions and I would answer them as best I could in the hopes that something I said would trigger memory recall.

34

"Ouch, that hurts!"

"Sorry," I said as I removed the electrode band from around his head. "The skin on your forehead is still tender. I'll be more careful next time."

He rubbed his head gingerly as Anna scurried about and came back with Plastiskin to spray on. "Here," she said. "This should take away the pain and protect it the next time they use the electrodes."

He looked at her and smiled warmly. "Thanks, Anna."

I turned away to keep them from seeing me smile. When I composed myself, I turned back and said, "Well, what would you like to talk about today?"

"Tell us about New Jerusalem. Anna told me about how the Moses found the ancient's laboratory over two hundred years ago. How he had the vision he should start the new version of Jerusalem following the description and laws from the Holy Book. But how did he do it? What has happened during those two hundred years?"

"Well, that's a very long and complex history," I said.

"Sorry," he said in a friendly tone, "maybe you could give us the short version?"

Even the short version took several days. I told them how the Moses and his small band of followers had explored the huge underground laboratory built by the ancients over three hundred years ago. How it took them several years to explore it all. I told him how they found the food storage areas, and power complex that offered a variety of renewable energy sources and energy storage devices. I described how they found the medical facilities and the weapon caches and so many other things, mysterious things they could not comprehend until they found the greatest discovery of all: the talking computer.

Anna, as well as the stranger, hung on my every word and I found myself going into greater and greater detail. As an indentured servant, Anna wasn't permitted to go to school so this was her first exposure to a complete story of the city's history.

"The talking computer was the key. They had been in the computer room numerous times, but they had no idea of the purpose of the strange shaped boxes that filled the room. Quite by accident, in the process of cleaning, the Moses himself activated the system. When the computer came online and began asking for instructions, pandemonium broke out. They all went screaming from the room, sure they had been infiltrated by a scavenger gang. When they finally returned after checking all the known entrances to the lab and finding them still secure, it still took them days to come to an understanding of what the computer was and its potential for establishing New Jerusalem."

The stranger looked puzzled. "So, New Jerusalem is just the ancient's lab?"

"Oh no. It's much more than that. The lab is mostly underground and heavily shielded by thick concrete walls. New Jerusalem is built on top of the lab. I'll show you a layout of the lab and the city tomorrow."

The next day after another failed attempt to stimulate his memory, I took them into my office. "Computer, show a layout of the ancient's lab."

The lights in my office dimmed automatically and a detailed drawing of the lab appeared on the rear wallscreen in red lines. I explained to them what each complex was for and how they were used in the construction of New Jerusalem. Then I explained the evolution of the city.

"New Jerusalem has been continually expanding since the first building was erected a hundred ninety-three years ago. Actually they built the inner Ring Wall first for security reasons, and then they built the Temple. As more and more people became Chosen, more rings were added. The Outer Wall is now the fifth ring. It was completed about twenty years ago."

As I spoke, the computer added the ring walls in different colors and showed all the details of the facilities built within each ring.

"Why are the gates offset?" he asked. "Wouldn't it be simpler for all the gates to line up? That way you could get from outside the city to the inner rings more quickly."

"The offset gates are for security reasons." I said. "You see, not everyone wants to become one of the Chosen, but many outside New Jerusalem would like to benefit from the fruits of our labors."

"You've been attacked?"

"Several times during the last one hundred eighty years. The last time was the worst; it was about fifty years ago. They actually broke through the outer wall and killed many of the Chosen before they could be driven off." I paused and remembered the stories my parents told of those chaotic days. "Everyone in New Jerusalem was afraid the city would fall and we would be back living like savages again. It was a terrible thought. But the security priest and protectors saved us. They brought out some of the weapons from the ancients' armory, terrible weapons of destruction, and killed all of the attackers."

"All of them?" asked Anna with a small shudder.

"Yes, Anna. Just like Joshua at the Battle of Jericho. We killed every single one of them; men, women and children. We drove them out of the city, pursued them across the waste lands and then we killed them. We killed them all as an example to others who might think of us as weak because we were civilized and lived ordered lives."

Security Priest Simon

It was taking too long, far too long, for this stranger to regain his memory. The entire secret of his identity hinged on him getting his memory back. The investigation was at a stand still. We had questioned everyone in Ring 3 that was close to the Gate 3N Plaza and most of what we got was worthless. I had the testimony of a four year old girl who saw, "an angel all dressed in blue float down from heaven on a sunbeam." She also said that her imaginary pet lamb ran away because the angel scared him. A wino said he saw "a man in a funny looking blue suit walk out of a bright light. Or maybe it was a red suit and he came out of a dark doorway."

Information I didn't get was just as bad. We checked all the records at all the gates from the Outer Ring to Ring 3 and the stranger wasn't on any of them. Someone suggested that maybe a tunnel had been dug under the walls and above the ancient's lab. We probed the grounds and got nothing but solid dirt and concrete.

I was convinced the stranger was a spy or part of an advanced guard for an army who was going to attack New Jerusalem. It could be that the only thing that restrained them was not knowing if their spy had been captured and if he had, how much information we were getting from him regarding their plans. But how long would they wait? I couldn't afford not to be prepared. I will not go down in history as the security priest who let New Jerusalem fall.

I walked into Senior Healer Johnson's office and took my usual seat. She stared at me and shook her head; I continued to glare at her. Her assistant came into the office and took a seat beside his boss. "Tell me you have made progress," I commanded.

"You won't like it," she said slowly.

"Tell me anyway."

"His condition remains unchanged, but there's more."

I waited as the senior healer looked down at her notes. She took off her glasses, sat back and rubbed her eyes with her knuckles. I noted in passing she looked exhausted, but that was immaterial. "I'm not sure the best way to say this, so hear me out."

I nodded and she began. "I have subjected the patient to every conceivable test in search of a way to speed the return of his memory. Most of the tests have been repeated many times by a variety of healers and their assistants. The results of the tests keep coming up the same."

She paused and I waited, but when she failed to continue, I snapped, "Is there a point to this somewhere in my lifetime?"

She seemed to become increasingly agitated and then burst out, "He's an alien, different from anyone I have ever seen before, or that any healer in New Jerusalem has seen in the last two hundred years."

I rolled my eyes upward and made a short prayer for the Lord to protect me from lunatics, and then pinned the good healer with my most withering stare. "Is that the best you can do? Is that all you can say after all the weeks you have been studying him, 'he's different?' Hell's fire, woman, I know he's different. Even the protector who stunned him knows he's different." I stood up from my chair with such force it toppled over, "I don't care if he's different," I said, ignoring the chair. "I just want to know where he comes from and what he's doing in New Jerusalem. I don't care if he's a mutation or from a long lost tribe that somehow survived The Plague or … or … or…" I turned in exasperation and shouted at Junior. "And what have you found out? Anything? Anything useful?"

Junior blanched and began to stutter, but I had had enough. I slammed my hand down on the desk. "Stop that noise and speak to me, man. Your life, the very existence of this city, may depend on what you know."

He swallowed hard a few times and then tried to speak. I picked up my chair and sat down as he cleared his throat and began again. "I've seen the patient twice a day for over a month. He's very bright and seems to grasp new concepts quickly, but he continues to claim he doesn't remember anything of his past. As far as I can tell he's telling the truth."

"Do you query the computer to be sure he's not lying?"

"Yes, SP. The computer would automatically notify me if he was lying."

I stood up and began pacing around the room; there had to be an answer here somewhere. They watched me pace but kept silent as I wracked my brain for anything that might help our cause. I turned to Junior. "Have you checked the calibration on the computer?"

Junior looked stunned. "SP, I'm a healer not a computer tech."

40

The senior healer interrupted, "The computer has been calibrated several times since the stranger arrived. There have been no reports of malfunction or drift."

I began to pace again, then stopped. "You said he was alien. Could it be possible the computer can't tell if he's lying?" They looked at each other and shrugged.

"I don't know, SP. But it should be a simple matter to check," said Junior.

"Perhaps after we're done here," I said and continued to pace.

I stopped in front of Junior and watched him squirm in his seat for a moment. "You said he was bright; how do you know? Have you given him any intelligence tests?"

Junior looked at Senior Healer Johnson hopefully. "We are scheduled to begin them tomorrow," she said.

She was lying. I didn't need a computer to tell me that. Neither she nor Junior had thought of it. I wondered what else they had forgotten. I turned back to Junior. "If you haven't tested him, how do you know he's intelligent?"

Junior shrugged his shoulders and started stammering again. I waited him out. "I … I guess mostly by the questions he asks … it's the way he asks them. It reminds me of the way a student questions an instructor."

I began to get a bad feeling about where this was heading. "Give me an example," I asked with a calmness I no longer felt. "What kind of questions does he ask?"

"Well, we were discussing New Jerusalem, its history and how it evolved. I showed him a layout of the ancient's lab and how the city was built on top of it. He asked why the gates to the rings were staggered and I. . ."

41

I stood up screaming, "Have you lost your mind?!! Are you a complete idiot? You showed a suspected spy the layout of the city … the location of the ancient's lab … the armory … the computer?"

The Stranger

I was frustrated. Physically I was fit. But I was making no progress when it came to my memory. I felt it was just out of reach, on the other side of a very thin wall that I couldn't quite penetrate. If it hadn't been for Anna, I think I would have lost my mind, the little that I had left. Anna was a breath of fresh air in my very restricted life. She seemed to be happy to be with me. To her, I wasn't an experiment, something to be poked and prodded to report back on a response measured. I was someone for her to talk with and apparently she hadn't had much chance to do that since she came to New Jerusalem. Indentured servants are property and treated as such; nobody talks to a chair or a table. But I was getting bored with living in the same small space. I was restricted to a few rooms in the hospital and I was getting closet fever. "Let's do something different today," I said.

"Like what?" asked Anna.

"Let's see if we can break out of the hospital," I answered with a grin.

She looked thunderstruck. "Are you out of your mind? The protectors would hunt us down and separate us. I'd never get to see you again," she wailed.

42

I hurried to comfort her. "It was a joke. I was only joking. It's just that I feel so confined. I want to get my memory back and get on with my life. I'm as anxious as the SP to find out what I'm doing here." I put my arms around her and hugged her gently.

She buried her head against my shoulder and said in a low voice, "I hope you never get it back. If you do you'll go away and I'll be all alone again."

"No I won't. I won't leave you alone, I promise. Whatever happens, we'll be together." I lifted her head and kissed her softly on the lips. I hadn't thought about it, hadn't planned it; it just happened. Suddenly, I knew I meant it. We were in this together. Right now, it was getting way too serious; I knew Nasty was monitoring us. I put my hands on her arms and backed away smiling then said, "Watch this!" I stepped back and fell into a back shoulder roll. As I came up, I jumped as high into the air as I could and kicked straight out, first with my right foot and then with my left. I landed lightly on both feet and did a series of rapid punches.

"What are you doing?"

"A kata," I said as I executed a rising block followed quickly by a reverse punch which flowed into a roundhouse kick. I stopped and looked at Anna who was standing there with her mouth open. "It's a kata," I said, "from karate. It's a way of practicing when you don't have any opponent."

"It's from your past," she said with a gasp. "You're starting to get your memory back!"

A cold chill ran up my back. I could remember the karate classes, taking tests for higher ranks, getting my black belt.

The door swung open, in stalked Nasty followed by Senior Healer Johnson and Junior. There were two protectors; both had their wands out as if they expected trouble. With no preliminaries Nasty started giving orders. "Put on your shirt and come with me."

"Where are we going?" I asked

"Senior Healer Johnson has certified you as being fit to stand trial for your sins," sneered Nasty. "You, and all involved with you, are to be taken to the judge." Nasty's attitude changed from frustration to confident arrogance as he motioned one of the protectors towards Anna. "Bring the slave girl too."

Judge Aaron

"All rise. The Superior Court of the Chosen is now in session, Judge Aaron presiding. You may be seated." The bailiff's monotone voice reminded me of a computer; devoid of emotion. And that was appropriate. For this is a court of law, emotions have no place. I looked down from my bench at the people whose fate I would decide today. They looked the same, just like everyday, sinners waiting to receive their punishment; praying for leniency, but knowing there would be none. The Law was the Law, and Law would be served.

One was different, an outsider, possibly a spy. And his eyes were brown, truly a hideous sight. There was the look of sin written all over him. There would be no leniency for him. Not for him with the evil brown eyes.

I stared at them all and said nothing. Stared with penetrating eyes until they started to sweat and squirm. All but the evil one. He sat calmly, hands folded in his lap and stared back with his cursed brown eyes.

I looked down at my case notes then looked up at the bailiff. "Proceed."

"On today's docket we have four sinners to be tried in related sins. Before we begin, Senior Healer Johnson wishes to make a statement regarding the physical and mental state of one of the sinners."

I nodded my head and a heavy set woman rose and approached the bench.

"Your Honor, I am the stranger's physician." She turned and pointed toward the man with the brown eyes. "He is recovering from a level eight stun that has left him with a memory blank. It is my considered opinion that any additional punishment at this time could result in the blank being permanent. In addition, if he is punished at wand settings greater than five it could result in the loss of his life."

I looked at the bailiff who quickly handed me a document. I scanned it and asked the woman, "If you do not feel that your patient is fit to stand trial, why did you sign this certificate?"

"Security Priest Simon said I had to."

"Now why would he say that? Aren't you the healer in charge of this case?"

The woman hesitated for a moment then continued in a stammering voice. "The medical computer indicated the patient would be able to stand trial, and the Law says that the computer evaluation is to be used as the final authority in such matters."

"I take it you do not agree with the computer."

"No, Your Honor, I do not."

I stared at her with a look of contempt on my face. "So what would you have me do Senior Healer? Leave his sins unpunished?" I asked scornfully.

"No Your Honor, but perhaps you could consider postponing punishment until he is more fully recovered." There was a quaver in her voice as she made her ridiculous plea.

"Why should I do that, Senior Healer? Why should I give this man special treatment?"

"Because he isn't one of us."

"I can plainly see the obvious, Senior Healer, but it is insufficient cause to delay justice."

"I'm sorry, Your Honor. I'm not referring to his physical appearance. He is not from Earth."

I looked at her in astonishment and then threw back my head and laughed. When I had regained control of myself, I said, "Senior Healer, I have heard many excuses in my twenty years as a judge. In fact, I had thought I had heard them all, most of them many times, but that is the most preposterous . . ."

"Your Honor, if I may continue?"

"Of course, I like a good fairy tale as well as the next person. Please continue."

"When the stranger was brought to my hospital, as part of his treatment we did a full analysis of his blood. This is standard procedure, especially in the case of severe burns and electric shock. When I looked at the results of the analysis I was surprised to find out that his blood did not contain any plague antibodies. We have repeated the analysis several times using different equipment, but the results were the same."

I was bored with this and showed my displeasure. "So you have concluded this proves he is not from Earth?"

"Your Honor, every person who has ever had their blood tested at New Jerusalem's hospital for the last two hundred years, and that includes all new born babies and everyone who enters through the Outer Ring Gate, has had The Plague antibody present in their blood. That amounts to several hundred thousand people. What other explanation could there be?"

"Are you saying he is not human?"

"No. He is human, but he is from a race that no longer exists on Earth. His ancestors must have left Earth before The Plague. What other explanation . . ."

"There could be a number of explanations, but let's assume you are correct. Let's assume that our young stranger is from ... oh, let's say the moon. He will still be tried by our laws."

"But think of the research possibilities. The opportunities to study . . ."

"Your request is denied, Senior Healer. Do not push your luck."

The stout woman looked disappointed, but then smiled grimly. "Would you consider releasing his body to the hospital for medical research if the punishment results in his death?"

"Of course," I answered amiably. "The court is not insensitive to the need for medical research. Well," I said in a cheerful voice, "let's proceed. Bailiff, who's first?"

"The Court calls Protector Graves," droned the bailiff.

A tall muscular young man approached the bench. The bailiff read the sin. "Protector Graves punished a sinner at an inappropriate wand setting resulting in extreme physical and mental injury. The sin called for a level one punishment; the wand was set at level eight."

I shook my head. "Protector Graves, this is a very serious offense. New Jerusalem has entrusted you with sacred power and you have misused it. Do you have anything to say in your own defense?"

Graves shook his head. "No, Your Honor."

I sighed. "You are to be punished with a level eight stun. Let the punishment fit the sin."

Graves' shoulders sagged briefly, then he straightened as two of the court protectors took his arms and led him to the punishment pad next to my bench. One of them stepped aside as the other unholstered his wand and thumbed the setting to eight. He was just about to lay the wand on Graves' shoulder when the stranger spoke up.

"Your Honor?"

Everyone turned toward the stranger who was on his feet, his yellow features seeming to pale at the course of the proceedings. "Yes?" I said in a menacing tone. "What do you want?"

"Your Honor, I don't understand why this man is being punished."

I sighed and looked heavenward as I prayed a silent prayer for the Lord to deliver me from legal amateurs. When I was done, I scowled at the man and said, "It is not necessary for you to understand. Protector, proceed."

"No, wait. I am the one who suffered as the result of his mistake. I should have some say in his punishment."

The young lady sitting next to him had hold of his sleeve and was attempting to get him to sit down and be quiet, but he shook her off and approached the bench. The court protectors moved to stand between us to protect me from any rash action.

The young man stared at one of the protectors and in a low voice said, "Careful, your wand is still set on level eight. You don't want to end up like your friend over there."

The protector quickly stepped back and reset the wand.

"Young man," I said, "you seem to be laboring under the delusion that you understand our law."

48

"No, Your Honor. I don't understand it at all." He gestured toward Protector Graves. "What happened was an unfortunate accident. I hold no feeling of malice towards him; I do not seek revenge. I don't want him to be punished."

"What you want is of little consequence. The Law is very specific in cases such as these. It makes no difference if it was an accident or if you do not seek revenge. A sin has been committed; a punishment will be made. Please return to your seat and remain there or I will find you in contempt of court."

Slowly he backed away, but I could tell he was having a difficult time accepting our ways. I have found this to be true with many of the Gentiles.

The two court protectors returned to Protector Graves and took up their positions. When I nodded my head, the wand was brought down on the sinner's shoulder. There was a loud electric snapping sound and Graves' body stiffened and then spasmed briefly. His hair stood straight out from his head and his eyes rolled back as he collapsed forward onto the pad. As I anticipated, he was unconscious. There was the faint smell of ozone in the air as I turned to look at the other sinners in my court. They were all sitting with their eyes downcast, hands balled into fists held rigidly in their laps, avoiding the sight of the punishment they too would soon be experiencing. The stranger was the only exception; he was standing with a wild-eyed look on his face. I ignored him.

"Senior Healer, would you be so kind as to check on the physical condition of Protector Graves?" I asked graciously. Then turning to the stranger, I said in a stern voice, "Please sit down and quit interrupting my court. Bailiff, next sinner."

49

As the senior healer attended to Protector Graves, the bailiff stood and read from his data pad, "The Court calls Citizen Sharon Gray."

A young woman in her mid-twenties approached the bench. She was visibly trembling, perhaps shaken by the sight of Protector Graves' punishment and his still unconscious body lying on the pad. Good. That was the purpose of punishment, to make people think twice before they sin, to make them aware of the consequences of their actions.

"Citizen Gray, you are charged with stealing a cape belonging to another citizen. Do you have anything to say in your defense?"

In a weak, faltering voice the woman started to speak, but I interrupted her. "If you intend to make a statement you will have to speak up. I cannot hear you."

The woman coughed to clear her throat and began again. This time she could be easily heard. "Your Honor, I did not steal the man's cape. I took it to help the stranger. I didn't know who or what he was, I only knew he was on fire and would die if I didn't help him. I've already replaced the burned cape with a new one. I beg of you, grant me mercy."

I stared at her for a moment and then, ignoring her plea, asked, "Did you ask the man for his cape?"

"No, Your Honor."

"So you took it without his permission?"

"Yes, Your Honor."

"Then, as defined by our Most Holy Law, you stole the man's cape."

"But, I used it to save a man's life!"

"So what? You still stole the cape, did you not?"

50

She was crying now, realizing her attempt failed and she would soon be punished. I spoke to the citizen in a sympathetic voice, "Because of the relatively low value of the cape and the fact you replaced it, I will give you the lowest sentence possible for this offense, a level three stun."

Two med techs entered the court and were putting the still unconscious form of Protector Graves on a power gurney. I looked at Senior Healer Johnson and she shook her head as she followed the gurney. A pity. Protector Graves had an excellent record up to this sin. Hopefully, he will recover sufficiently to still serve some function to New Jerusalem. If not, it was the Lord's will.

I motioned to the court protectors to take the woman to the punishment pad. As they took her arms, she collapsed into pitiful sobbing and they had to drag her to the pad. "Please don't hurt me. I was only trying to save him. Please, I beg of you . . ."

"Silence," I thundered. "You will take your punishment like an adult without this childish whimpering or I will increase the wand setting." The sobbing subsided as I knew it would and the protectors were about to proceed when the stranger interrupted again.

"Your Honor, this is not fair. You're punishing this woman for saving my life."

"You will return to your seat and be quiet." I was seething. "The next outburst by you will cost you a level one stun."

He chose to persist. "Let me take her punishment. If it hadn't been for me, this wouldn't be happening to her."

"That is totally irrelevant. She stole the cape; she is the one to be punished."

"Isn't a human life is worth more than a cape? Isn't it infinitely more valuable?"

51

"Of course it is, but that is also immaterial, and as I promised, you are hereby charged with contempt of court and will have a level one stun added to any other sentence you receive. Now, sit down and shut up!" I motioned to one of the court protectors to stand behind the stranger. "If that man says another word, I want you to stun him. I will have order in my court."

The woman stood trembling on the pad. Her eyes were tightly shut as the protector laid the wand on her shoulder. There was a **pop** and the woman let out a high pitched shriek and sank to her knees. She was sobbing loudly as a med tech escorted her from the court.

The bailiff stood and announced the next case. "The court calls Servant Anna. She is charged with disobeying a security priest and with moral misconduct."

The young woman sitting next to the stranger had a look of disbelief as she slowly stood. "I didn't do anything wrong. I didn't commit any sin. I just did what the healers told me to do."

The stranger attempted to take her hand and pull her back down, but the protector standing behind him laid a hand on his shoulder to restrain him. The girl was escorted to the bench as I read over the charges. "These charges are vague and incomplete. Who filed them?"

The bailiff nodded in the direction of SP Simon who was now also approaching the bench. "Your Honor, I apologize for the incompleteness of the charges. If I may, I would like to expand."

I sat back and glared at him for a second. "I don't like sloppy work, SP. You know correct procedure and I expect you to follow it."

52

"Yes Your Honor. But in this case I beg the court's indulgence. I was only made aware of the sins of this person as we were in route to the court."

"Very well. You may proceed."

The SP turned toward the terrified girl. "You are Servant Anna, indentured servant to Senior Healer Johnson; is that correct?"

"Yes sir," she answered in a voice weak with fear.

"And you were given the task to look after the stranger, were you not?"

"Yes sir."

"Who gave you that responsibility?"

"It was Junior Healer Murphy. He said Senior Healer Johnson had told him…"

"What were your duties?" he interrupted.

"I was to be like his nurse. To make sure he was all right, to bathe him and call one of the healers if he had any problems or if he started to get his memory back."

"Were you instructed to sing to him?"

The girl blanched and hung her head. "No SP."

"In fact, didn't I specifically tell you not to sing to him?"

The girl looked close to panic now. "Yes SP, but I thought it was just when you were visiting."

"Did I say 'stop singing when I visit' or did I say, 'stop singing?'"

"But…"

"But nothing. What did I say?"

With a bowed head the girl mumbled something I couldn't hear. "Speak up young lady. What did I tell you?"

"You said to stop singing."

"And did you?"

The girl looked up, her eyes were dead and her voice flat and devoid of emotion as she answered, "No, I continued to sing except when you or the healers were in the room."

There was a satisfied, almost smug look on the SP's face as he said, "So you admit your sin of disobeying the direct order of a security priest?"

The girl nodded slightly. "Yes SP."

SP Simon paused for effect and then his voice became ominous as he said, "Now for the more serious charge of moral misconduct."

He turned so he could look at the stranger as he continued, "How old are you, Anna?"

"I'm not sure, 18 or 19. I was born a Gentile and was brought to New Jerusalem when I was around 13."

"And what is your current status?"

The girl looked at the SP with the same dead eyes. "You already know what my status is. Why don't you just get this over with?" she said quietly.

I banged my gavel down loudly. "That will be quite enough of that attitude, young lady," I said sternly. "You will answer the SP's questions without any backtalk."

She stared at me for a long second then seemed to shrug her shoulders and turned toward the SP. "I have been indentured to Senior Healer Johnson for almost six years. She bought my contract the first week after I entered the city as an orphan."

"Are you married?"

"Indentured servants are not permitted to marry."

The SP paused and stared at the stranger. Without taking his eyes off of him he asked, "Then since entering New Jerusalem you have never seen a man naked, have you? Because it is against our Holy Law for an unwed woman to see a naked man."

The girl's voice was still flat as she answered. "I have seen the stranger naked. I was instructed by the healers to bathe him daily."

The SP fained shocked as he responded, "You mean to tell me you not only saw him naked, but you *touched* his private parts as well?" The SP had never taken his eyes off the stranger since he started this line of questioning. I glanced at him myself at this point expecting to see him highly agitated, but whatever the response the SP was trying to elicit was not present. The brown eyed man sat quietly, staring at the ceiling, apparently lost in thought. After a few seconds, the SP shook his head and turned toward the bench. "I have no further questions, Your Honor."

I looked at the two healers and shook my head. They should have known better than to have an unmarried girl tend to a male patient. They would have to pay for their own sins.

"Servant Anna, you are found guilty on both charges, but since these are your first sins, and since there seems to be some mitigating circumstances, I will grant you minimum punishment. You are to be punished at a level four wand setting. Protectors, please administer the punishment."

At this point, the chaos began. Even in retrospect, I am not exactly sure what happened or even what I saw but I will describe it as best I can. It began with a sound, not unlike an animal's roar. It was deep and resonant at the beginning, but quickly scaled up to the screech of a banshee. It came from the direction of the stranger. As I turned to look the first thing I saw was the protector, who had been standing behind the stranger, flying through the air. He landed on his back in the middle of the floor in front of my bench with a sickening crunching sound. My eyes were immediately drawn to the stranger who appeared to be flying out of his seat. He vaulted over the rail, took two quick steps that closed the distance between himself and the closest protector in a fraction of a second.

He then leaped straight up to an incredible height. At the same instant, his legs seemed to shoot out until his entire body was horizontal. Again the animal scream and again the sound of flesh being battered as his foot made contact with the side of the protector's head. The force of the kick lifted the protector off the ground and sent him soaring over a railing and into some vacant chairs where he lay quite motionless.

The stranger was anything but motionless. Like the most graceful of dancers I have ever seen, he landed lightly on his feet and turned toward the protector who was just starting to react. He had his wand raised about his head and you could hear the hum and crackle of a high setting as he rushed at the stranger. But instead of retreating, the stranger made a sideways skipping motion, screaming all the while, and drove his foot into the protector's midriff before he could land a blow. The kick sent the protector crashing into the wall and, as he bounced off, the stranger grabbed his wrist, somehow avoiding the wand and with a twist of his body, sent the protector flying one way and the wand the other.

It was at this point SP Simon got in the act. He attempted to grab the stranger by the neck, but it was like trying to grab a wraith. The stranger took a step back and the SP attempted to strike him with his fists, but the stranger avoided the blows quite easily which seemed only to infuriate the SP. He charged the stranger with flailing arms but was stopped suddenly by a blur of punches that moved so quickly they were impossible to follow.

There was yet another animal scream and the SP went rigid. The stranger stepped aside as the SP fell face down onto the floor. He moaned once through bloody, swollen lips and then slipped into unconsciousness.

To my great dismay, it wasn't over yet. Like a marionette on strings, he seemed to fly to the top of my bench scattering papers and important documents. I tried to stand up, to escape from this mad man, but he snatched the collars of my robe with a crossed arm grip and was pressing his forearms into the sides of my neck. I could feel myself losing consciousness as he pulled me toward him. We were only inches apart and I was staring into his wicked brown eyes. The last thing I remember was him saying to me through clenched teeth, "End this insanity."

The Moses

I had watched the trial in fascination, especially the way the stranger tested the judge. However, I was confused by His physical display. It was truly superhuman. That must have been it. He was showing me that He was a superhuman. Or maybe He was giving me a sign that it was time for us to talk. I watched the monitor and saw Him lower the unconscious form of Judge Aaron gently into his overstuffed chair. Then He began looking slowly around the room as if He was searching for something. Nobody else in the room was moving. Everyone was either unconscious or in shock. The entire fight had taken less than a minute and so far no one else had entered the court room.

He spotted the camera and spoke to it. I felt a chill run up my spine as He said, "I will talk with you now. The girl comes with me."

I gave orders to the protectors that no one was to challenge Him. He left the court, but first went to the hospital. When He emerged, I noticed He had shed His hospital clothes and put on His jumpsuit. It glistened as the sunlight bounced of the light-blue material as if it were made of metal instead of fabric. Taking the girl's hand in His, they headed for the Temple.

No one tried to stop Him; no one came within several hundred feet. However the protectors and SPs followed His every move. He must have seen them as they walked down Solomon Drive towards the Temple, but He gave them as much attention as a man gives an army of ants that happens to be nearby. From time to time, they would pause and He would ask the girl something. I should have been able to hear them with the sonic pickups, but for some reason all I got was static.

At last they reached the Temple. They stood outside and it appeared as if the servant girl was explaining the offerings that were burning on the altar. As she talked, He surveyed the Temple grounds with a critical eye. At last they entered into my chamber. Naturally, I prostrated myself on the floor in front of Him.

His voice was soft and low, but I could detect a hint of His power as he said, "What are you doing? Get up."

I kept my head bowed as I got to my feet. I noticed that the girl was standing behind Him, using Him as a shield. By the look on her face and the way she clung to Him I could see she was terrified by everything that was happening. But there was something more; she was awed by the Temple and being in the presence of the Moses. Only a few of the Chosen are ever permitted inside my Temple office. It was also obvious that she had no idea who the stranger was.

"Why were you bowing down to me?" He asked in a curious voice.

"To show my respect for the Lord my God," I answered with my head still bowed.

He looked puzzled. "What makes you think that I'm God?"

I looked at him fully now, surprised by the question. "Are you still testing me?" I asked. This was not going as I had expected. When He didn't answer, I shrugged my shoulders and said, "The Prophets have written that a Messiah would come to deliver His Chosen people. They said He would be different from other men with incredible powers."

His face broke into an ironic smile. "Well I'm different. That's for sure."

He began to walk slowly around my chambers, looking at the tapestries and gold-clad furnishings. The girl still hung to His arm, making darting glances around her at all the riches dedicated to God. She never once looked at me. He stopped in front of the Holy Book. He bent closer and looked through the glass. The inert atmosphere had helped to preserve the pages, but the ravages of time were still taking their toll. It was difficult to read, but I saw His lips move as He read the passage from Exodus where God was showing Moses, the original Moses, the Promised Land.

"How much of it remains?" He asked quietly, almost reverently.

"The Holy Book that the Moses had when he founded New Jerusalem had thirty-four books. Not all of them were complete. In the two hundred years that have passed, some of the pages have crumbled to dust or rotted away. We didn't know how to preserve the paper pages and print until about a hundred years ago and it was a very old book by then. Of course, it was scanned into the computer as soon as we understood how the scanning system worked. We have it all on file, but only parts of thirteen of the books from the original remain. Only the book of Exodus is complete."

"Did you try searching the computer for the Bible?" the stranger asked. "I'm sure there would be a copy in the computer memory."

"Yes, of course we did. It does show up as an existing file, but that portion of the computer memory is corrupted. Much of the memory was destroyed over the years before the Moses stumbled across the lab. Some by scavengers, but also a lot was lost to normal deterioration."

I turned towards the computer screen. "Computer, please display the passages from the Holy Book that deal with the coming of the Messiah."

The words began to scroll up on the screen and I watched Him as he read them. "Computer, stop."

He turned towards me and in an unsettling tone asked, "If you believe I am the Messiah, why were you so cruel to me and to those who were trying to help me?"

I fell to my knees and begged his forgiveness. "My Lord, I did not know who you were. I began getting reports from the SPs about potential invaders. They were sure you were a spy for an invading army, it wasn't until I saw you in the courtroom that I understood who you truly were. Please forgive us."

I stayed on my knees, but raised my head to see His face. It chilled me to look at His expression. I quickly lowered my head again and asked in a shaky voice, "My Lord, if you wanted to be treated like a king, why did you come like an invader? Surely you must have known how we would react. We follow your Laws very precisely and your behavior gave us no choice."

"Ah yes, the laws." His voice had a hard, sharp-edged ring to it. "Let's talk about your laws."

"But my Lord," I interrupted. "They are not *our* laws, they are your Holy Laws from the Holy Book." Something was wrong here, terribly wrong, and I could feel the fear begin to rise in me.

"Are they? Are they really? Are they all from the Holy Book?"

I started to answer, but He held up His hand to quiet me. The slave girl had let go of His arm and backed away from Him. She understood little of our conversation, but it was clear she was shocked at the way He was talking to me. After all, I am the Moses.

"If I remember correctly," He continued, "there are a little over six hundred laws written down in the Holy Book. Where is it written that a servant girl may not disobey an SP's order? Where does it say electric shock wands will be used to punish sinners? Just how many laws does New Jerusalem have?"

The feeling of fear was growing stronger. Somehow, someway, we had offended the Lord. I didn't know where this line of questioning was going, but I was sure I and the Moseses before me had committed some grievous sin. We had misinterpreted the Holy Word and I was going to be punished for it, punished as no other sinner had ever been punished.

"Answer me! How many laws do you have?"

I stammered, "I ... I'm not sure ... several thousand ... ma, maybe ten thousand laws. I could get the exact..."

He exploded in anger. "Ten thousand laws? You have ten thousand laws? And what is the result of having ten thousand laws?"

61

I was stunned. What was happening here? And then in a flash it came to me. It was a test! He was testing me again. Oh joy! I knew the answer to this question. I was positive I had the correct answer. A sense of well being and confidence swept over me and I got to my feet.

With my head still bowed I answered. "The purpose of the Holy Law is to show our devotion to the Lord's will. By following His laws we do what is right and holy in His … your eyes. We do this because we are your Chosen people. You have promised us that as long as we follow your Holy Laws you will protect us and keep us from our enemies. Many years have passed since the original Holy Laws were written and we have found it necessary to augment the Holy Laws to accommodate the world as it is today. But each law that has been added has been done so only with the intent of following the path you have set before us."

He stood silently looking at me. The girl had moved back to Him and had rested her hand on His shoulder. I did not approve of her familiar attitude. It appeared He did not seem to mind. He kept staring at me as if He expected me to say more. One final thing occurred to me. It was the clincher that proved my premises.

"And the correctness of this path we have taken," I said in a strong voice, "is proven out by the fact we have had peace and prosperity for nearly two hundred years." I couldn't help but feel proud of myself. I had met the challenge.

He continued to stare at me, His expression unreadable, however I wasn't worried now. I was confident I had given Him the correct answer. Finally, He spoke. "Yes, you have had peace and prosperity for two hundred years, but it has cost you your humanity."

My confidence began to unravel. What was He saying?

"You have your ten thousand laws and by enforcing them you have created a well ordered society, in doing so you have killed all human compassion."

"I don't understand." I trembled. "Isn't this what you wanted?"

He looked at me and shook His head. There was great sadness in His eyes. As I watched, tears began to form and flow down His cheeks leaving wet trails in their wake. He made no attempt to wipe them away and then He turned from me and I felt my heart break. I had made the Lord cry.

I fell to my knees and placed my forehead on the marble floor. "Please forgive us, Lord. We did what we truly thought was right."

I heard Him mumble something and I strained to hear it as He said it again. At last he turned to me and said, "You have no love, no compassion for your fellow man. You have only your laws, your ten thousand laws, and they have destroyed your love."

"That's not true," I said, forgetting to whom I was speaking. "We have love. We have love for you and for your Law.

"No!" He answered angrily. "Everything I have seen here tells me no. I came to your city and you almost killed me. I was a stranger who did not know the ways of your precious laws and you almost killed me for that. Then a woman saves my life while I am burning to death and she is punished for her troubles. Do you think she will ever again lend a helping hand to someone in need?"

I had put my hands over my head to protect me from His words that fell like heavy stones.

I prayed He would stop, hoped He would leave me in peace, instead He said, "Your healers think of me as some type of lab rat to experiment on. Your SP thinks I might be a threat so he would rather have me dead than take the time to find out the truth. To the judge, it was just another day at the office. The pain and suffering he doles out means nothing to him."

He put His arm around the girl who was trembling from His latest outburst to soothe her. "And this girl, this beautiful, innocent, loving child was to be punished for nursing me back to health … and for singing a song."

"But my Lord, the Law…"

"I am not you Lord!" He shouted at me and I cringed at the impact of His words. "The Messiah came over two thousand years ago … He was killed by people much like you."

What was he saying? He was not the Lord? Could this be true? "Computer, is He lying?"

In an instant the computer responded. In its inhuman voice, it said, "The stranger is telling the truth. He is not the Messiah."

The scene was a frozen tableau for what seemed like an eternity. I became aware of a keening, like from a wounded animal. That sound was coming from my own mouth. I began to tremble, then shake. I crawled to my knees and finally stood. Grabbing my robes in both hands I began to tear them from top to bottom. My face flushed in rage and I screamed the word that filled my mind. "Heretic!!! You cursed Heretic!!!"

He put up no protest when the protectors led him and the girl away. They took them outside the Temple to the stoning pit. It took no time at all for the Chosen to arrive and select their stones. I stood on the balcony above the pit and pronounced the judgment. "For the sin of heresy you and the servant known as Anna are sentenced to death by stoning. And may God damn your souls to hell for all eternity for what you have done to his Chosen people."

64

At this point there are mixed opinions as to what happened; the people at the edge of the pit were not in a good position to see. I was on the balcony and saw it clearly.

The girl clung tightly to him and he put one arm around her. He reached up and touched a stud on the neck of his jumpsuit and looked towards the sky. He seemed to be praying, perhaps asking for forgiveness, but I felt no compassion for him.

The Chosen surged forward towards the lip of the pit, their stones held high. At that instance, I saw a pale column of light descend out of heaven. The light engulfed them both as the stones began to strike, but it was as if the sunbeam were made of metal; the stones bounced off without striking them.

They began to rise into the air, slowly at first, but then faster. Within a few seconds they disappeared from view. The Chosen dropped their stones and turned toward me, but I had no words for them. I turned and stumbled into the Temple. I fell to my knees and began to wail. It had been another test and I had failed again. I had failed the test and the Messiah had left.

"What have I done?" I cried. "Dear God, What have I done?"

I must have fallen asleep there on the Temple floor, just inside the balcony door. The protectors and Temple slaves must have been too afraid to approach me and put me to bed. But something had woken me. I stirred, sat up and looked around. The doors were still opened and the balcony was bathed in a column of light. *He's returning,* I thought to myself. *The Messiah is coming back!* I scrambled to my feet and ran out onto the balcony and stared up into the light. It wasn't the Messiah, but something was coming down the beam. It was small and wrapped in the same blue cloth as His jumpsuit. When the package touched the ground, the light went out and I was once again in darkness. I picked up the package and took it into the Temple to my chambers. I carefully unwrapped it and took out the book inside. I sat down at my desk and read the inscription on the cover: In bold, large print it said **The Holy Bible**. A subtitle was written below in slightly smaller print, **Both Old and New Testaments**.

I opened the book. On the inside of the cover were two notes. The first one read:

To the crew of the Generation Ship Hope
May Captain Noah guide his Ark to a New Promised Land
May God sail with you and guide your way.

The second note was written in a different hand:

To the Moses of New Jerusalem
May you find the truth
The truth will set you free

I turned the page and began to read.

Part 2
The Generation Ship *Hope*

GENERATIONS

68

Lieutenant Hiroshi Koyama

Anna and I continued to ride the light beam back to the ship. I could tell she was scared to death by this experience, but there was nothing I could do to comfort her. It would all be over soon. She gripped me so tightly, I could hardly breathe. I had both my arms wrapped around her and once the beam was activated there was no possibility we would fall.

I leaned my head back and looked up and could see the sky was turning black as we reached the end of the atmosphere. Inside the light beam it was like standing on a platform. There was little sense of motion or outside sound at all. Through the magic of technology we could breathe normally.

I looked down at Anna; her eyes screwed shut. "Try to relax. It won't be long before we're on my ship. We're safe now. No one is going to hurt us. Why don't you open your eyes? I guarantee you are going to love the view. You'll be the first person on Earth to see this in two hundred years."

She turned her face into my chest and I could barely hear her muffled voice. "You promise it's not scary?"

"Yes, I promise it's not scary. You can't fall. Just open your eyes and take a quick peak. You won't regret it."

She turned her head slightly, just enough so that if she opened her eyes she would be able to see a spectacular view of Earth and millions of stars in the sky above. As I watched her closely, I could see she barely opened her eyes just a sliver for just an instant and then closed them tight. But I could hear a deep intake of breath. Then she opened them fully and turned her head to see more of the view.

70

"Oh my!" she exclaimed and turned her body until her back was against my chest and she could see the full panorama. "It's so beautiful. I've never seen anything like this. Thank you so much for showing me this."

She turned back around. We were facing each other, my arms loosely around her waist keeping her secure. She raised up on tiptoes and kissed me passionately. "Thank you for saving my life, thank you for caring about me. Thank you for my first kiss." She snuggled against me, but suddenly stopped. She began laughing, giggling at first, but rapidly turning into a hysterical laugh. She stopped and leaned back, looked at my face and said, "I love you dearly, but I don't even know your name! Please tell me you're not called 'Stranger.'"

I laughed with her for a moment and hugged her tightly against me. "What's wrong with Stranger? I kind of got used to it while I was in New Jerusalem." We laughed some more and kissed again and then I told her, "My name is Hiroshi Koyama. I'm a lieutenant in the Space Navy." I looked up and saw my ship growing rapidly bigger. "Soon we'll be entering my ship. Her name is *Hope*. It will take some getting used to. It won't be like anything you've ever experience before."

Anna got suddenly serious. "Will we be together? Please tell me we'll be able to be together."

"Always," I answered as we entered the ship through the Beam Room Hatch.

Captain David Lawrence

We all waited expectantly for Lieutenant Koyama to board. It had been the better part of a month since he had left to reconnoiter the city we had discovered. We lost contact with him almost as soon as he touched down and many of us feared for his life. He reported that he was bringing a local woman who was seeking sanctuary. Hiroshi indicated she would be an incredible source of information. The command crew was very anxious to hear their debriefing.

Hiroshi and the woman stepped out of the beam onto the platform. The platform was surrounded by an invisible isolation screen that protects the crew from any possible biological contamination. He was holding the hand of this young woman. He faced me, came to attention and snapped a crisp salute. "Lieutenant Hiroshi Koyama and guest request permission to come aboard, sir."

I also came to attention and returned the salute. "Permission granted, Lieutenant. Could you please introduce your guest?"

"Yes sir, her name is Anna. She is my fiancée."

I couldn't help notice the look of shocked surprise on the young woman's face followed by the biggest smile I had ever seen. "Welcome aboard, Anna. Congratulations to you on your betrothal."

I turned back to the rest of the crew in the crowded room and said, "Please listen up." The room immediately became silent. "I know all of you can't wait to personally welcome home Lieutenant Koyama and Anna, however we are required to follow contamination prevention protocols. This is for their protection as well as ours. In a few minutes they will be escorted to Dr. Song's med bay for examination. Once that has been successfully completed, they will be quarantined in their quarters for at least twenty-four hours. As soon as the quarantine is lifted they will begin briefing us on what happened in New Jerusalem. In the evening, 1800 hours ship's time, one day from today, we will hold a welcome home party in the crew's mess. Duty rosters will be adjusted so every crew member who wishes to attend will have at least two hours to visit with them. Any questions?" There were none. "Let's get back to work. Dismissed."

The transport vehicle pulled up to the platform and I watched as two hazmat med techs helped Hiroshi and Anna off the platform and into the vehicle. The doors were closed and sealed. The vehicle moved into the transport tube and began its trip to the med bay.

Doctor Soo Song

I watched as the transport vehicle came to a stop and the doors opened automatically. A guide robot met them as they stepped from the vehicle and said in its electronic voice, "Please follow me." They followed the bot into the isolation chamber where I stood waiting.

"Good morning. Welcome to my med bay. Hello lieutenant, nice to see you again." I turned to the attractive young woman and said, "And this must be Anna, your fiancée. Lieutenant Koyama has gone through this procedure several times before, but for your benefit, Anna, let me give you a quick overview of what we are going to do. You will both lay down on your separate examination beds where all of your vital signs will be monitored, recorded and evaluated. A blood draw will be made by one of our med bots and a very thorough analysis of your blood will be performed by our computers. It should not take any more than thirty minutes. Assuming everything is normal, you will then be escorted to your quarters for a twenty-four hour quarantine period. All food will be provided, delivered to your quarters. Would you prefer separate quarters or would you like to share?"

Before the lieutenant could answer, Anna said, "We'd like to share, please." I noticed the lieutenant smiled and shrugged his shoulders.

All testing was successfully completed. They re-entered transport vehicle which took them to their quarantine quarters.

Anna

The door to our suite automatically opened, then closed and locked behind us after we entered. I turned and jumped into Hiroshi's arms and kissed him madly all over his face. "I can't believe this is happening," I said as I laughed. "We should be dead, covered in stones and damned forever. But instead we are in a fairy land of brown-eyed people, wonderful, friendly, beautiful people, in this spacious suite of rooms. This is just too much for Servant Anna to absorb.

"Do you want to know the absolutely best part of all of this? I am finally alone with the man I love, a man who loves me, a terrific kisser, by the way. I can't believe you told them we're engaged." Then a thought crossed my mind, maybe he introduced me as his fiancée so they would let me onto the ship. Maybe he doesn't really want to marry me. He just wants to protect me.

He noticed the change in me and asked, "What's the matter, Anna. What are you worried about?"

"Are you sure you want to marry me? We've only known each other for a month. Maybe you've got a girlfriend on the ship you love more than me. Maybe…" I couldn't keep the panic out of my voice. Maybe all this *was* too good to be true.

His voice was soft and calming. "Anna, I knew from the moment I heard you singing to me, before I was even fully conscious, I wanted to be together with you. When I finally woke up and learned how compassionate you are, when I kissed you the first time, I knew I loved you. Riding up on the light beam to the ship, I decided I wanted to be with you for the rest of my life. I have no girlfriends on the ship. Sure, I have friends who are women, but I don't love them. I love you. I want to be married to you as soon as we can arrange it."

His words filled my heart with so much joy, I began to cry. I put my arms around him and pulled him close. He stroked my hair and kept saying, "Don't worry, Anna. I truly love you. You will be my wife soon, very soon."

I don't know how long we stood there, just holding one another, but when we stepped away, I felt more calm than I had ever felt in my life. All my fears had melted away.

He took me by the hand and said, "I want to show you something." We walked across the living area to a wall-to-wall curtain. He said in a commanding voice, "Computer, open curtains."

The curtain parted and opened up on a floor-to-ceiling window, revealing an incredible view. At first, I couldn't tell what I was looking at, but then it snapped into focus. It was a panoramic view of a world turned inside out. It was like a miles long barrel, miles in diameter, with fields, farms, villages, forests, rivers and lakes all laid out on the inside of the barrel. I looked above me and my first question was, "Why doesn't the stuff on the top of the barrel fall down?"

"The barrel is slowly spinning which acts like gravity. Everything is pushed back against the barrel walls. We don't feel the spin because it's slow and steady, but it gives the same effect as gravity on Earth," Hiroshi explained.

"What are those two big lights for, the ones floating on the center line of the barrel?" I asked.

"Those lights act like small suns. They produce light and heat to simulate daylight. We need the light to make the crops grow and other things. When it's supposed to be night time, the lights go dim and the stars come out. You'll see them tonight."

"Will you take me out there sometime? I'd really like to see what it feels like to walk on the surface of an inside-out world."

"Of course, my love," he answered. "As soon as our briefings are over, we'll go visit. I spend a lot of my work time out there. Perhaps you can travel with me on some missions."

There was a soft chime at our door. We turned from the window and Hiroshi looked at the ID screen next to the door. "It's our dinner," he said. "Feel like eating?"

"Yes," I answered. "We haven't eaten all day, I'm really hungry."

"Me too," he replied and pushed the Enter pad next to the door and it slid open. A moving table covered with wonderful smelling food drove into our room and stopped in the middle of the empty space next to the window. Chairs extended from either side of the table and we sat down. A soft woman's voice asked, "Would you like music with your meal?"

I bent over to look under the table to see where the woman was hiding, but Hiroshi stopped me. "It's the table's computer speaking. We're quite alone. Would you like to listen to some music while we eat?" Hiroshi asked.

I didn't know what to say. I'd never listened to music other than my own singing, and it's hard to eat and sing at the same time. I decided to leave it up to Hiroshi. "Whatever you'd like, my dear."

"We'd like some soft instrumental music please, not too loud," Hiroshi ordered and we began to eat as the most beautiful music I had ever heard filled the room.

It was the best meal I had ever eaten. It tasted wonderful. It didn't matter that I had no idea what most of the food was. The aroma of every dish was like being in a perfume shop smelling all the delightful fragrances. But the taste and texture of the food was unlike anything available in New Jerusalem. We didn't eat too much, but I was pleasantly full, and then something called dessert magically rose from the center of the table and I could not resist. What a fabulous ending to what started out as the worst day of my life, what I thought would be the last day of my life.

Hiroshi served up what he called an after dinner drink. It came in something called a brandy snifter, a very large bulbous glass with a warm brown liquid in the bottom. Hiroshi showed me how to swirl the warm liquid around in the glass and then stick your nose inside the glass and breathe in deeply. After the first few sniffs, I began to feel ever so relaxed.

We moved a piece of furniture in front of the window. It was like a small sofa, built for only two people. He called it a love seat, and I quickly found out how it got its name.

We sat looking out the window and watched the two sun lamps slowly dim into two moon lamps. As it got darker, the stars came out and began to twinkle. The lights from the villages and homes began to twinkle as well. It was so romantic. We sniffed our brandy and took a sip or two. On the third sip, Hiroshi kissed me and let his drink slide into my mouth. It was the most pleasurable thing I'd ever felt. I kissed him back in turn and we shared brandy and kisses until all the brandy was gone.

He picked me up and carried me to the bed. I fell asleep in his arms holding him tightly against me, so much in love.

Lieutenant Hiroshi Koyama

I awoke the next morning to the sound of water running in the shower. I opened my eyes and looked around the bedroom. Ship's daylight was shining through the smaller bedroom window. The door to the bathroom was closed and I could hear the faint sound of Anna singing in the shower. I sat up in bed and yawned as I stretched my arms. I noticed I was still wearing the same clothes they gave me at the med bay. I got up to see if they had stocked the closet with other clothes. As I opened the closet door, I heard the shower stop along with Anna's singing. I was looking through the selection of clothes when Anna came out of the bathroom wearing a white robe and her hair wrapped in a towel.

"Good morning, my soon to be husband. I trust you slept well." She walked over to me and gave me a hug and a kiss on the cheek. "Do you need to use the bathroom, brush your teeth, or take a shower? I know, how about I bathe you like I did back in New Jerusalem? I know how much you liked that," she said as she began to laugh. "Here, let me help you take off those old smelly clothes."

78

She reached for the drawstring on my pants, but I took hold of her hand and laughed with her. "I think I can handle my own hygiene, at least for today. But I may take you up on that bath in the near future. Thank you for your offer."

"How about you order breakfast for us, then take care of your hygiene? Oh, what do I do with the clothes we were wearing yesterday? I can't seem to find a hamper."

"There is no hamper. The clothes they gave us in the med bay and here in the quarantine quarters are incinerated. It prevents the spread of any illnesses we might have brought with us from New Jerusalem. They are made of paper for better disposal. Just wad them up and throw them in the trash bin."

She looked at me to see if I was joking. When I didn't respond, she gathered her clothes from the bathroom and stuffed them in the trash bin and went to the closet to choose her new wardrobe for the day. I ordered breakfast and took care of all my bodily needs, dressed, and joined her in the living room just as the breakfast arrived.

We sat by the window again looking out at the inside-out world as we ate. She said to me, "I have so many questions to ask you. When I got up this morning, I came in here and looked at the world and kept asking myself, why would you need your own world on a space ship? I bet you know the answer, because my future husband is very smart and strong and an excellent kisser."

"Okay," I said as I spread strawberry jam on a piece of toast. "Let's just keep that part where you say I'm an excellent kisser between you and me."

She leaned over the table with a pretend scowl, "You think I'm a fool? Do you think I want any other girls to know what a great kisser you are? Then they'll all want to try you out and I'll have to stand in line to kiss my future husband. By then, your lips will be all chapped and swollen. So I'm not going to mention it to anyone."

I couldn't help laughing at her comments. I stood up and threw my napkin onto my chair as if I were angry, walked around the table, grabbed her by the hair and pulled her head back, and kissed her full on the lips. It was a long, passionate kiss. When it ended she said, "Wow! I'm definitely not going to tell anyone what a great kisser you are. This morning your kiss tasted like brandy and strawberry jam."

I returned to my seat, retrieved my napkin and said, "Enough about kissing. Let me tell you about *Hope*, the second of the generation ships. Generation ships were built to travel to locations very far away from Earth. The distance to the closest star, Alpha Centauri, is a little more than four light years."

"What's a light-year?"

"A good question, my darling. Our sun is ninety-three million miles away from Earth. It takes light from our sun eight minutes to reach Earth. A different way to say it is, the Earth is eight light minutes from the sun. Alpha Centauri is four light *years* from Earth, that means the light from Alpha Centauri takes four years to reach Earth. Our fastest ships can only travel a small fraction of the speed of light so it would take us close to a hundred years to get to Alpha Centauri and another hundred to get back, around two hundred years for a round trip."

"Why not go somewhere closer?" she asked.

"One of *Hope's* missions was to discover Earth-like planets. There are a total of eight planets in our sun's system. Only Earth is compatible with human life. Almost three hundred years ago, scientists on Earth discovered a planet they called Proxima B orbiting a star called Proxima Centauri, one of the three stars that make up Alpha Centauri star cluster. They thought Proxima B might be able to sustain human life. Decades of further study confirmed the possibility. A series of very high-speed drone probes were sent to gather on-site evaluation. It took ten years for the probes to reach Proxima B and four years for the results to be transmitted back to Earth. The data substantiated that Proxima B could sustain human life with very minimum terraforming.

"What's terraforming mean?" Anna asked.

"It means taking an alien world and making it very similar to Earth. Examples would be changing the atmosphere so we could breathe it without wearing masks or helmets, modifying the soil so it could grow Earth type crops, those types of changes.

"The only way to get to Proxima B is in a generation ship. The original crew that left Earth all died before the ship was halfway to our destination. It took two generations of descendants from the original crew to reach Proxima B and another three generations to return."

"Why couldn't they build ships for humans that could go as fast as the probes? That way you could be there in ten years instead of a hundred."

"Another good question, Anna. I can tell you've given this some serious thought. The answer is complex. I really don't understand the science of it, but let me try to answer."

She poured him a glass of water and said, "If you don't understand it, how do you think a poor, uneducated, dumb servant girl like me has any chance? But please try. I love to hear the sound of your voice when you're being all serious."

I took a sip of water, and said to her, "You may not have gone to school, but you are not dumb by any definition of the word. I can tell by the questions you ask that you understand quite a bit." I paused for a moment and then said, "Would you like to go to school? When I am working and you can't be with me, you could be learning how to read and write. Would you have any interest in that?"

She got up, ran around the table and sat in my lap. "You are a mind reader, my love. I have been worrying that I am not good enough for you. I was picturing myself walking down the street with you. And the smart girls we pass are saying to each other, 'There goes that incredibly smart and very handsome Hiroshi with his dummy of a wife. What a shame, he could have done so much better.'"

I knew she was teasing, but I could tell there was some concern on her part that some of the crew would truly have those types of thoughts. I kissed her on the cheek and said, "If you truly want to learn, I will make sure you have the opportunity. And I will use a wand at a level eight setting on any woman who even hints of those terribly thoughts."

She kissed me back and whispered in my ear, "Thank you for everything dear man. A level two stun would be good enough." She returned to her chair and I finished my story. "The drones travel at more than half the speed of light. At that speed, running into a grain of sand can be disastrous. The drones had shields supposed to deflect everything in their way, but they were not always successful. We sent out ten probes, only two survived the trip. They took their data and transmitted it back to Earth. Shortly afterwards they shut down. That's why we needed to build a generation ship. *Hope* was built to provide as close to an Earth-like environment as possible for all our generations as we travel."

Anna thought for a few seconds. "That must have been very expensive. Why would anyone want to spend so much money for something that would take so long to complete?"

"The best answer is survival. The survival of the human race. The construction of *Hope* began twenty years before The Plague came along. Many years earlier the corona virus of 2020 was a worldwide pandemic that resulted in millions of deaths and the near collapse of the world's economy. It took over a year to come up with a vaccine. A lot of people began wondering what else could wipe out the world's population? There had been a number of recent extinction events that had threatened the world. There were reports of potential large meteor strikes, global warming that would result in worldwide flooding, other natural disasters, like earthquakes, hurricanes, tsunamis, volcanoes, and the ever present possibility of nuclear war.

"A worldwide movement began with plans of how to preserve the human race. They tried colonizing our moon and Mars, and considered terraforming the large moons of Jupiter and Saturn as possibilities, but all those options had serious drawbacks. The moon and Mars established scientific bases but they never grew into colonies. Orbiting space habitats were considered and a few were built, but one was destroyed by orbiting space junk. Over ten thousand people died in less than a minute. Future projects were abandoned and the other habitats evacuated."

Anna

We took a bathroom break and looked out the window at the world below. Hiroshi found what he called binoculars. I had never seen anything like them before. When I looked through the small eye pieces at the fields below, they looked like I was standing in the middle of the field. I had to hold them very still or the image seemed to jump around. Hiroshi also found a stand that he could attach the binoculars to holding them steadier.

As I was looking at the countryside and marveling at the sight, Hiroshi was looking around our suite. I heard a man's voice behind me, I turned quickly when I realized it wasn't my Hiroshi. There was a large screen on the wall showing pictures of the inside-out world. The man's voice I heard was the narrator.

"What did I miss?" I asked Hiroshi.

"Nothing, I'll restart it in a minute." He turned toward the screen and said, "Screen pause." The image on the screen froze and the narrator stopped talking.

"I think you would really like to see this. It's an introduction to *Hope.* It touches on everything in the ship and how it works. Do you want to see it?"

"Of course," I said. "Will you watch it with me?"

"Yes, but I'm going to do a karate workout while I watch. If you have any questions, just say to the screen, 'screen, pause.' When you want to start up again, say, 'screen, resume.'" He went into the bedroom and took off his shirt and stepped out of his slippers. When he came back to the room he looked toward the screen and said, 'Screen, play from beginning.'"

I could hear soft music playing as the outside view of the *Hope* filled the screen. The background was as black as night with more stars visible than could ever be seen in the night sky from New Jerusalem. It seemed like we were circling the ship, first on top and then underneath. There were very tiny little creatures crawling on the outside of *Hope*. They looked like small multicolored bugs, but as the camera zoomed in the bugs became people. I realized the ship was enormous, perhaps bigger than the entire city of New Jerusalem.

I paused the picture and turned to comment to Hiroshi, but stopped to admire his physique. Of course, I had seen it before, but now he looked somehow different, different in a good way. There didn't seem to be an ounce of fat anywhere on his upper body. When he moved, the muscles seemed to ripple underneath the skin. His movements were like a blur, incredibly fast. When he locked out a technique his muscles seemed to swell in size, as if he had pumped fluid into them from a hidden reservoir inside his body. He stood very still for a second, every muscle tensed. It reminded me of the chart Senior Healer Johnson had hanging in her office; the one with the skin stripped away revealing every individual muscle.

He looked at me and relaxed. "Something wrong with the screen?" he asked.

"What? oh, nothing. Nothing's wrong." I was embarrassed and excited at the same time. I turned back to the screen and said, 'Screen, resume.'"

The video showed me everything I wanted to know about this generation ship and more. For example, the term crew applied only to the people who operated the ship. That amounted to about one thousand people of the total five thousand ship's personnel. The remaining four thousand were scientists, farmers, ranchers, doctors, dentists, teachers, professors, and every other type of occupation you can imagine in a typical small town on Earth. The non-crew passengers had their own government. The title of their leader was Governor.

When *Hope* left Earh orbit there were only four thousand on board. Half of them were married and the other half engaged. People were selected based on the needs of the ship. People with multiple skills had a better chance of getting selected. Most of the applicants were single when they applied, but it was subtly suggested they might consider getting married to another highly rated single applicant of the opposite sex. It was suggested their chances of getting selected were significantly improved for a married couple, both with mutiple skills and already pregnant.

For the newly married and not yet pregnant as well as the single applicants, you had to be willing to have children. It was expected that there could be as many as a thousand births the first year. After that, you had to wait for someone to pass away before you could get pregnant. The total population of the ship had to be maintained very close to five thousand. If it got too high, there wouldn't be enough food to feed everyone.

The ship had to be self sustaining. It had enough food to feed the passengers and crew for the first year. After that, they had to live on what they could grow. That included fruit, vegetables, grains, cattle, pigs, chickens etc. There would be no deliveries of supplies once they left Earth's orbit

Everyone had a job to do. Actually, each person had many jobs to do. Multitasking was a way of life. Everyone worked until they weren't capable of working. At that point, they became instructors preparing the next generation to take over their previous work responsibilities. There were not a lot of choices for the next generation to make. They were slotted into jobs based on the needs of the ship and their qualifications.

I paused the video. Hiroshi was done with his karate workout and had gone to take a quick shower. The twenty-four hour quarantine was almost over and I didn't want him to visit Dr. Song with a bad case of man smell. I ordered us a light lunch as Hiroshi had shown me and the soft chime indicated it had arrived. Hiroshi came out of the bathroom smelling like a man should smell just as the table propelled itself near the window. This had become our favorite place to eat. I don't think I will ever get tired of the view.

We had an hour before the transport would pick us up. We ate slowly. Hiroshi had asked me to order sushi, a traditional Japanese dish. He began eating with two sticks instead of a knife and fork. He said they were traditional Japanese eating utensils. He made it look so easy, but I managed to flip my first bite onto the floor. I was so embarrassed. I ate the rest of it with my fingers. Hiroshi said I would learn to master chop sticks quickly.

We finished lunch and were getting ready to go. I mentioned to Hiroshi, "I'm really going to miss this place, especially the view. Where will we end up living?"

"I like this place too," he said. "I used to live in an area known as the BOQ, Bachelor Officer's Quarters. But since we're getting married soon, I requested this suite to be our permanent residence. In the meantime, you'll be living in the single women's dormitory."

I frowned. "But I want to be with you. I don't want to be with a bunch of women."

"I want to be with you too, but until we're married, we can't do that. Being quarantined together was a one-time deal."

The door chimed and slid open. Our transport was waiting.

Doctor Soo Song

Their transport arrived promptly twenty-four hours after they were placed in quarantine. They made such a nice looking couple. More importantly, they looked like the picture of health. Hopefully, their test results would confirm their well being. "Good morning to you both," I said, returning Anna's smile. "I hope being locked up for twenty-four hours with the lieutenant was not too confining?" I said, teasing them a bit.

The lieutenant smiled back at me, but Anna had a very wide grin on her face as she said, "Oh my goodness, no! It couldn't have been more perfect. The suite, the view of the inside-out world, the food, the music, all of it was wonderful. It was the first chance we've had to be alone and relax without fearing somebody was going to throw rocks at us."

"I'm so glad you liked it." Then I frowned slightly, "What is the inside-out world, please?"

The lieutenant answered for her. "It's what Anna calls the inside of the ship's barrel. To her it looks like a world turned inside out."

"*Ah* so. Actually, a very good description." I gestured toward the examination room and said, "Are you ready for your final examination?"

They nodded and headed for the room. The follow-up exam to check their vitals and run comparative blood tests was quickly completed followed even more quickly by the data analysis. Only one item was found that I needed to discuss with Anna. We sat in my office as I went over their test results.

"Lieutenant, you'll be happy to know you did not pick up any strange bugs from your stay in New Jerusalem. Your brainwave patterns are identical to the tests we took before you rode the beam down. Tell me, have you been having any headaches, or migraines? Any residual memory loss that you are aware of?"

He shook his head. "No doctor, I feel fine."

I turned to Anna. "Of course, we have no data to compare you to, but everything we measured is in the normal range. There is one antibody in your blood that is not familiar to us. Are you aware of that?"

Anna thought for a moment before saying, "I think that is related to The Plague. I've heard the healers in New Jerusalem say that everyone who survived The Plague has that antibody present in their blood."

"Were you ever given a vaccine shot to protect you from The Plague?

"I don't think so. Listening to the healers makes me think it developed naturally when we were infected." She paused for a moment then added, "I'm not sure if this is important, but only people with blue eyes survived The Plague. All the people with brown eyes died from it."

I looked at the lieutenant who nodded his head and said, "That's right, Dr. Song. I forgot to mention it, but that's why they were afraid of me. They thought I was some kind of alien because my eyes were brown. Is it important?"

"I'm not sure, but I'll check on it."

I stood up and they stood with me. "You are both cleared to go. I understand you will begin your briefings now. And the welcome home party begins at 1800 hours."

Anna asked me, "Will you be at the party, Dr. Song?"

"Absolutely, barring any emergencies, I'll see you both then."

They boarded their transport and where taken to the main conference room.

Governor John Stewart

The conference room was beginning to fill up. Captain Lawrence and I had agreed to limit the attendees for the briefing to those who had a vested interest in what happened at New Jerusalem. Of course, in the interest of complete transparency, the meeting would be broadcast throughout the ship.

The plan was to have Lieutenant Koyama give us an overview of what happened to him at New Jerusalem and then open it up to questions from the attendees. I have to admit I'm not comfortable having Lieutenant Koyama's guest present for the entire briefing. I know it is unlikely, but there is the possibility she is a spy for the New Jerusalem government.

All of my people were already seated and Captain Lawrence, his executive officer, Commander Henry White, and select members of his crew were just sitting down. I noticed the captain's wife, Miriam, was also present. When the transport from the med bay pulled up, the lieutenant and his guest joined us. Since they were both considered members of the crew, they sat next to the captain.

I stood and the briefing began. "Ladies and gentleman of the Generation Ship *Hope*, today we welcome home one of our own. We feared he was lost to us and, it turns out, he nearly was. Not once, but on two occasions. Seated beside him is his guest. Her name is Anna and I believe she is largely responsible for nursing him from a near-death condition to full health. We all owe her our thanks for her efforts. Today's meeting is scheduled to last no longer than four hours. Lientenant Koyama, we would appreciate it if you would give us an overview of your experiences in New Jerusalem for the first thirty minutes. I'm sure there will be many questions for you and Anna that will follow. Additional meetings are anticipated to determine our go-forward strategy. Do we stay focused on the New Jerusalem site or do we move on and search for a more hospitable facility to complete our repairs and upgrades? Lieutenant Koyama, you have the floor."

The lieutenant stood and told his story. Everyone in the meeting was hanging on his every word. It was so exciting, yet terrifying at the same time. It reminded me of listening to my grandfather tell us bedtime stories when I was a small child.

He ended with the comment, "If Anna had not nursed me back to health, I don't think I would be alive today. Even if I had survived, I probably would never have regained my memory. I can't thank her enough for all that she did for me."

The meeting attendees stood as one and gave her a standing ovation which seemed to embarrass Anna a great deal, but she grabbed the lieutenant and hugged him tightly which seemed to delight all those present. When everyone quieted down and took their seats, the chaplain raised his hand.

"Yes Chaplain, you have the floor," I said.

Chaplain Byron George

I stood and faced the group and began. "First of all, let me thank the lieutenant for that amazing account of his stay in New Jerusalem. I'd like to expand on his story regarding what he did after returning to *Hope*. After hearing his story, the request he made of me now makes perfect sense. I need to give some background of how New Jerusalem is governed. They are a theocracy based on the Old Testament of the Bible. Apparently, they didn't have access to even the complete Old Testament. They do have a complete book of Exodus and a substantial portion of Leviticus. Their laws seem to be focused on these two books. In many ways, they became like the Jews just before the coming of the Messiah. They are ruled by a man known as the Moses who resides in a Temple at the center of the city. He is the absolute ruler of New Jerusalem and his rule is based entirely on Old Testament Law. Unfortunately, just like the Jews, they 'augmented' the six hundred and thirteen Biblical laws with additional ones until they had accumulated over ten thousand laws. Before we departed on our mission in *Hope,* the Jews had recorded similar additional laws into a book called the Talmud.

"The Moses had a sufficient portion of the prophetical Old Testament books to be aware of a Messiah coming to save the Chosen. They seemed to believe the lieutenant met the Biblical description of the coming Messiah. They were very upset when he denied his divinity. The Moses claimed he was a heretic and ordered him to be stoned to death, along with his accomplice, Anna. After they were beamed out, the lieutenant requested we send the Moses a complete Bible with both Old and New Testaments. We were happy to send this leader a copy of the official ship's Bible. We beamed it down to him the next morning. I believe we attempted to contact New Jerusalem numerous times without success. It appears they have no communications capability beyond very short range, personal com units. Due to the needs of restocking and repairing *Hope,* it was decided to send a representative from the ship to establish contact and to determine if they were capable of assisting us. As the lieutenant just presented to us, we have a problem. They may have the ability to assist us, but they may not have the will. Apparently, they know nothing about the generation ships that were launched prior to The Plague, and consider anyone from outside their walls a threat. I would like to suggest a next step. I would like to send them a communication system down the beam and begin a dialog with them. We should be able to safely and quickly determine if New Jerusalem has the ability to assist us, and if they would be willing. I would also recommend that Lieutenant Koyama be the one to attempt to communicate with the Moses. I'm certain their leader would be very interested in finding out why the stoning he ordered failed. If he is successful and they are willing, we can include other crew members as appropriate. We need to consider what we would be willing to offer them in exchange for their help. I yield the floor."

Quartermaster Geoffrey Taylor

I raised my hand and the governor granted me the floor. "I concur with the chaplain regarding beaming a vid com system to the Moses of New Jerusalem. I believe we should continue to explore the possibilities of them being able to help us. For those who may not be aware, New Jerusalem is built on top of what they call 'The Ancients' Lab.' When we began our mission, approximately ten years before The Plague, the lab was known as Oak Ridge National Laboratory. Oak Ridge was the main source of supplies and equipment when *Hope* was being built and it makes sense for us to return to this location. Once we have an operational vid com system in New Jerusalem we should be able to access the lab's computer system. If we're successful in that regard, we can determine if the supplies and equipment we need to refurbish and repair *Hope* are available. I believe our needs are critical. As of today, we have less than a month's worth of reaction mass. Granted, we are in orbit now and are not using our EM drives, but we're running low on almost everything. By my estimate, we have no more than two months of consumables left. In light of that, I would recommend we consider a parallel activity to our actions with Oak Ridge. What comes to mind is using our shuttles to investigate the other DOE national lab sites, to see if they can be an alternative to Oak Ridge. When we broke orbit for Alpha Centauri, there were twenty national labs in America. I know that Los Alamos and Sandia Labs supplied the Generation Ship *Faith*. There are other possible lab sites in Europe, Asia and South Africa, but I recommend we look at the ones closest to us first. Governor Stewart, I yield the floor."

The governor stood and said, "Quartermaster Taylor. I agree completely with your assessment." The governor turned and addressed the captain. "Captain Lawrence, I think we should put together a committee to plan our actions for evaluating the other American lab sites. Do you agree?"

"Absolutely, governor. We could use the rest of the time today to pick group members and get started on the plan. I would also like to put Lieutenant Koyama in charge of getting the vid com system beamed to the Moses and start discussions on that front. Are we in agreement on that item?"

The governor stood and said, "Yes we are. I can think of no one better qualified than the lieutenant to head up that operation." He turned to the rest of the room. "Let's get busy, people. Don't forget the Welcome Home Celebration at 1800 hours. Captain, may I speak to you a moment in private?"

Lieutenant Hiroshi Koyama

Our part of the meeting was over. I took Anna by the hand and led her to the chaplain to make introductions. I thanked him for his recommendation and told him I looked forward to working with him on contacting the Moses.

Our next step was to talk with the quartermaster to requisition a vid com system. He directed me to one of his assistants who took care of getting everything we needed including instructions on how to operate the equipment. It was all packaged up for transport and sent to the Beam Room. I checked with the Officer in Charge to determine when our orbit would take us over New Jerusalem. He said we had about an hour.

On our way out of the conference room, the XO called to me, "Hiroshi, wait up." He and Miriam were making their way toward us. "We wanted to introduce ourselves to your fiancée."

Anna took one look at the XO and took a half step back. I had to admit, the XO is … unique I guess is the best way to describe him. He was about six feet tall and weighted close to three hundred pounds, all of it muscle. He was the official heavy weight power lifting champion of *Hope*. His best lifts were record setters: five hundred twenty-five pound bench press and nine hundred fifteen pound squat. His total for the three competition lifts was over a ton. In spite of his size, he was a pussycat. When he shook Anna's hand he did it softly. He could be serious when the situation demanded, but most of the time, he was fun to be around. One ensign had said, "The XO is a party waiting to happen."

Miriam smiled as she shook Anna's hand and said, "Welcome to *Hope*. After hearing how you saved Hiroshi, you are my hero. I know everything must be new for you. I'd like to get together with you soon, just the two of us, for coffee. Can I com you in a day or two?"

Anna was delighted. Dr. Song was the only female she had met since coming aboard. She was friendly, but was very busy with her job. Here was a chance to have a new friend she could hang out with when I was tied up with work. Anna was all smiles as she chit chatted with Miriam and said she'd love to get together for coffee, maybe in the upside down world. Miriam looked over at the XO who also looked confused.

"That's Anna's name for the farm land," I said.

"A perfect name. I'll call it that from now on," said the XO as he smiled at the two women.

I took Anna to the officer's mess to compose a message for the Moses to read when he received the vid com system. On the way, I could tell something was troubling her. I asked, "You don't seem happy. What's up?"

She stopped walking, turned to me and said, "What's wrong with the XO?"

That surprised me. "Nothing's wrong that I know of. What did you notice that I missed?"

"Several things," she answered. "His skin is really dark, his hair has very tight curls, lots of things like that. Was he burned or is he just extremely tanned?"

I stood silently trying to figure out what she meant, finally it dawned on me. I said to her, "Anna, the XO is a descendant of a race of people who originally came from a continent called Africa. When *Hope* left Earth orbit there were over a billion people whose skin was just as dark as the XO's. My skin is darker than yours and my eyes are shaped different because my ancestors came from a continent called Asia. Most of the people from Asia and Africa are born with brown eyes. You told me The Plague killed almost everyone with brown eyes. It probably killed almost all of the people with Asian and African ancestry and that's why you never saw anyone with dark skin. Out of the five thousand people on *Hope* , many hundreds, maybe thousands, of them have their roots in Aisa and Africa. Dr Song's ancestors are also from Asia just like mine. You are going to see a lot more dark skinned people. But nothing is wrong with any of them. They are just as smart as you and me, they think like we do, they just look different."

Anna finally smiled and said, "You are so smart, I think you know everything. You always have good answers to my questions. I'm so glad the XO is all right. I was afraid he was in great pain from a fire."

The officer's mess was almost empty when we arrived. We got a couple of pieces of fruit and cups of coffee and sat by ourselves in one corner of the mess hall. As I was setting up to compose the message to the Moses, Anna bit into the apple she had picked up. Her eyes went wide as the juice leaked out around the corners of her mouth. "This tastes so good," she said as she covered her mouth with a napkin. "It's so juicy and sweet. Were these grown in the inside-out world?"

I smiled at her and said in a teasing voice, "No, we picked those up this morning from a produce store in one of New Jerusalem's suburbs. Glad you like it."

She wadded up the napkin and threw it at me. "I'll take your snotty answer as a yes. I'm just so impressed that you grow everything you eat and have been doing it for so many years."

"It's not just the food. We make our own clothes and shoes, soap and toothpaste, replacement parts for when machines wear out. We recycle our water and waste. Almost nothing is thrown away. Unfortunately nothing last forever. *Hope* was designed to last for two hundred years. We're over that milestone by eleven years now and we won't survive much longer without help.

"We found out about The Plague ten years after we left Earth's orbit. We had already left our solar system. We considered turning back, but the leaders at that time decided to continue on to the Alpha Centauri system. After all, that was our mission, to make sure the human race survived. If we turned around there really wasn't anything we could do to help. Earth had many medical experts working on it and they couldn't find a cure. We just hoped there was something to come home to when our mission was over."

"Why didn't you stay at … what was that planet called again?"

"Proxima B," I said. "And some of us did stay. The mission was clear; if we found Proxima B to be able to sustain human life, some of us would leave the ship and set up a colony. I wasn't even alive then. I was born on the return voyage home. In fact we were only twenty-five years from Earth when I was born."

"How many people stayed?" Anna asked. "Were they chosen before you left Earth?" She paused for a moment then corrected herself. "I guess the people who stayed on Proxima B wouldn't have been alive when *Hope* left Earth."

"Very good," I said. "You're learning to think like someone from a generation ship. To answer your question, just under two thousand people stayed. We had equipment stored onboard that was dedicated to the colony. If it turned out that Proxima B was not suitable we had a few options. Fortunately, Proxima B *was* suitable. We were in orbit around the planet for one Earth year. Everyone had the chance to visit the surface and to decide if they wanted to be part of the colony or start back to Earth. We had many volunteers to stay on Proxima B. Those chosen were selected based on filling the needs of the new colony as well as the needs of the ship returning to Earth."

We finished up our message to the Moses, polished off the fruit, drank the coffee and headed for the Beam Room. We put the message in with the instructions for the vid com system, watched the techs load the package wrapped in the blue transport material and then saw it start its journey down to the Temple balcony. It was a short trip. When the time was up, a confirmation signal was received. They had the package.

It was time for the Welcome Home Party.

Captain David Lawrence

I made my way to the crew's mess hall along with many well wishers. The lieutenant was very popular and for good reason. As the head of ship's security, he had the unenviable job of maintaining peace among our diverse inhabitants. He had the reputation for being friendly but fair. He played no favorites and showed no tolerance for anyone who tried to take advantage of others.

When he was promoted to lead the security detachment, he was the youngest ever to hold that position. He knew that had ruffled the feathers of some of the more senior members of security. He approached each one of them separately and when he was through, there were no more ruffled feathers.

Being a sixth degree black belt in karate and also holding the rank of black belts in judo and aikido hadn't hurt his popularity. One of his first activities after assuming the lead position was to organize martial arts tournaments and training sessions for men, women, seniors, and children. He sold it as a great physical and mental fitness activity and initially led all the classes at least once a week.

At precisely 1800 hours, the party began. The crew's mess was jammed with friends and well wishers from all over the ship. All crew members were attired in their dress uniforms. We don't wear them often, but this was a very special occasion and justified the wearing of our monkey suits.

When Hiroshi and Anna entered everyone stood up and cheered. The music began and so did the toasting. As tradition demanded, after every song, one of the ship's officers would ring a bell to signal silence and make a toast. It began with the lowest ranking ensign and worked its way up the chain of command. I would be the last to toast and that would signal the end of the party.

One special musical attraction was the karaoke medley performed by the Asian members of our crew. Apparently, you only had to have one distant ancestor of Asian blood to be considered eligible to perform. There were group songs and solos, upbeat songs and sad ballads, some were sung in English and other in various Asian languages. The medley finally wound down, cueing the last toast of the evening. The last performer was Doctor Soo Song. She also held the rank of commander and had given the next to last toast just before she began singing a song she introduced as a famous Korean battle song.

Everyone was surprised to see the good doctor begin to take off her uniform. Underneath she was wearing a traditional Korean dress that was not only beautiful, but bordered on the risqué.

100

Many of the crew appeared shocked the very conservative doctor was letting her hair down.

The song began as a slow, very sad dirge. Her voice was soft and low, you could see a tear or two forming in her eyes as she finished the first movement. But suddenly, the tempo changed. The music became louder with a stronger beat and screaming brass, the commander's voice echoed the music. Her movements became more animated. As the music approached the climax, she began screaming as if she were fighting in hand-to-hand combat. She began a series of Taekwondo punches and kicks, jumping and spinning kicks as she ripped off parts of her clothes. With the final clash of the symbols she collapsed onto the floor in a heap. It was the most incredible performance any of us had ever seen.

Everyone had been cheering her on as she danced and sang, but when she fell to the floor and the sound of the clashing symbols faded away, the room became silent. There was concern that she had injured herself, but gradually, slowly, she began to rise, first her head, then her shoulders. She gathered her feet under her and rose to a standing position. As she began to move, the applause began. By the time she was standing up, it was a thunderous ovation of clapping, cheering and people calling her name. She was drenched in sweat, her jet black hair matted against the sides of her face, her makeup in complete disarray. But she began smiling, raised her hand and waved, then bowed slowly from the waist. When she came out of the bow, the room began to chant her name: "Song, Song, Song…" She looked radiant as she bowed again then turned and moved to the edge of the room.

I waited until she was out of the center of attention and the murmur of the crowd faded. I moved up onto the platform for the final toast. I looked at all the smiling faces. It had been a great welcome home party. "I'm supposed to give the final toast of the evening, but how can I ever come up with a toast that could compare with Commander Song's performance? Wasn't she fantastic?!!" As I finished speaking, the good doctor grinned, caught getting back into dress uniform again. The crowd began chanting her name and she looked embarrassed as she gave small bows.

"I would like to ask our guests of honor to join me on the platform, please."

Hiroshi and Anna stepped up onto the platform and waved at the cheering crowd. I gestured to the governor and said, "Governor, would you also join us?"

Governor Stewart stepped up with us and stood on the other side of the couple. Hiroshi looked outstanding in his dress uniform, However Anna really stole the show with a beautiful dress, hairstyle and makeup. I could tell Miriam had been busy helping Anna's transformation from a servant girl to a beauty queen.

"Before I offer my toast, I have a few announcements. I'm sorry to say the first one is on the negative side. You requested certain quarters for you and your fiancée. Unfortunately, those quarters are reserved for married couples and one of them has to have the rank of at least lieutenant commander. Since you are not married and neither of you have the rank of lieutenant commander, we have to deny your request."

I noticed that Anna momentarily looked disappointed, but her smile returned quickly. "For the next announcement, I would like to turn the platform over to our governor. Governor Stewart, would you do us the honors?"

"I'd be happy to, captain." He reached inside his coat pocket and brought out a purple, velvet box and opened it. He faced Hiroshi and said, "Lieutenant Hiroshi Koyama, for your courage in combat and the injury you received while on a mission within a foreign government, I, as representative of the Generation Ship *Hope,* would like to award you the Purple Heart." He pinned the medal on Hiroshi's left breast.

He turned to Anna and said, "Anna, for your courage and perseverance in nursing our lieutenant back to health and risking death for your actions, I, as representative of the Generation Ship *Hope,* would like to award you the Legion of Valor Medal, it is the highest honor given to a civilian."

Hiroshi was stoic in his appearance, but Anna looked shocked. However, her shock didn't keep her from smiling as the governor pinned the medal to her dress. The governor turned to the captain and said, "Thank you, captain, for allowing me to participate in this award ceremony."

He stepped down from the stage area and I turned toward the lieutenant. "I have one other award to make. Actually, it is not an award. Lieutenant Hiroshi Koyama, based on your time in rank and for outstanding performance not only in your assigned duties, but also for the extra assignments you volunteered for, you are being promoted from lieutenant to lieutenant commander, effective this date."

I removed a box from my pocket and took out two gold oak leaves. I gave one to Anna and I took the other. We removed the two silver bars from each of his shoulder epaulets and pinned on the gold oak leaves. Hiroshi came to a rigid attention stance and gave me a crisp salute. There was just a trace of a smile on his lips, but Anna had the biggest smile I had ever seen.

They turned to face the cheering crowd. "Just one more thing before the toast. I'm sure you can't wait to get back to work, but this is important." There were a few moans and fewer laughs as I continued, "Color Guard, front and center. Miriam, you will be the maid of honor and I will be the best man. Dr. Song, you will be the bride's maid, Commander White you will be the groomsman. Where's the chaplain?"

Doctor Song came running around the Color Guard holding three beautiful bouquets of flowers in one hand and a bridal veil in the other. She handed Anna one bouquet and one to Miriam while she kept the last one. She reached up and placed the veil on the bride's head.

The chaplain stood at the middle of the platform as Hiroshi and Anna turned to face him. Anna was trembling so hard I was concerned she might fall down and motioned to her maid of honor to stand close to her just in case. The chaplain began, "Dearly beloveds, we are gathered here in the sight of God to join together this man and this woman in holy matrimony…"

When it came time for the exchange of rings, I handed the new lieutenant commander a diamond ring we made that morning. Miriam had one for Anna to give to the groom.

"I now pronounce you man and wife. You may kiss the bride," said the chaplain and they turned and faced the crowd who had begun to cheer wildly. *The Wedding March* began playing as they walked between the ranks of the color guard holding crossed swords above their heads.

As they walked out of the crew's mess, the quartermaster greeted them, "Congratulations you two. Since you were recently married and promoted, your request for certain quarters has been changed. Here are key cards to your new suite. God bless you both."

The room began to empty and the clean up detail came in to prepare the crew's mess for dinner. I walked over to Soo Song and congratulated her on her performance. We chatted briefly and I found out she had studied both dance and martial arts while becoming a doctor. She held a second degree black belt rank in Taekwondo. I thanked her for filling in as a bride's maid.

Most of the people had left the mess hall and I took Miriam's hand and we began to walk toward the exit, when it dawned on me, *I forgot the last toast!*

Lieutenant Commander (LCDR) Hiroshi Koyama

I have never felt such joy in my entire life. Life is so strange. Two days ago I was standing in a pit waiting to be stoned to death by a mob of angry fanatics, and today I've been presented with a medal, promoted in rank, and married to the woman I love. God truly works in mysterious ways. I opened the door to our new quarters, but we didn't go in right away. I mentioned to Anna the old tradition of a husband carrying his new bride across the threshold of their home the first time she entered.

Anna said it was a silly tradition, and besides she had already crossed the threshold when it was our place of quarantine. She began to say something else, but I picked her up in my arms and ran inside, spinning her around and around as she squealed and laughed with her arms tightly around my neck. She began kissing me all over my face, hundreds, maybe thousands of little tiny kisses all over until she stopped at my mouth and gave me a proper kiss. I don't know how long we kissed but eventually I lowered her to the ground. We stood there in the darkened room with only the light from the two moon lamps and artificial twinkling stars, shining through the picture window. It was so beautiful. I had seen this view hundreds of times through other windows, but this time it was different, more beautiful, more meaningful. Sharing it with Anna made it a very special moment.

However the mood was broken when the table said in a very sultry woman's voice, "Congratulations you two, would you care for a glass of champagne? It's been chilled to perfection with a taste that is a bit brash, but not obtuse."

Anna gave a short scream when the table began talking and I have to admit it startled me too. Anna leaned over and whispered in my ear, "I'm going to kill the woman hiding under the table. By the way, what does obtuse taste like?"

I kissed her on the cheek and answered, "I have no idea what obtuse tastes like and if there is truly a woman hiding under the table I will help you kill her. Computer, soft lighting, please."

The light came on and we walked to the table and raised the tablecloth. No woman. I think Anna was disappointed. I quickly checked out the suite to make sure my so called friends hadn't planned any other pranks on us.

We opened the bottle of champagne and each had a glass and a piece of very good wedding cake. After a second glass of champagne, Anna was looking kind of dreamy. We sat together in the love seat and she snuggled up to me and said with a slight slurred voice, "The table was right, the champagne was not *too* obtuse."

I picked her up in my arms and carried her into our bedroom and lay her on the bed. She smiled up at me and reached up and pulled me close and kissed me. "I love you so much, my darling husband. Come sleep with me. I need you."

I will not go into detail about what happened the rest of the evening. The Navy says I am an officer and a gentleman and a gentleman never discusses his intimate relations with his wife, thank you very much.

The Moses

It was late. I had been up poring over the Bible they sent me. Ever since it arrived, I canceled all routine meetings. I still presided over Sabbath service, but other than that, I told my servants I was not to be interrupted unless it was an extreme emergency.

I believe I was the only one to see the Bible coming down the beam of light. It was so late in the evening, I'm sure everyone was asleep. It was the light from the beam that woke me. Of course, I believed it was not really a holy book, but some type of fraud; an attempt to divert my beliefs. I spent hours comparing our limited copies of what they called the Old Testament against their books and was shocked to find they were an exact match. I was even able to match the numerous fragments of unknown books we possessed and identified them as coming from books we never heard of. This led me to the conclusion their complete Old Testament was not a fraud since they had no way to know what fragments we had. I was convinced they had a genuine, complete, and intact testament of all thirty-nine books.

What then could I say about the other testament, the New Testament? There was an index at the beginning of each testament, listing the names of books and grouping them into related categories. For example, in the Old Testament, sometimes referred to as the OT, the first five books are called the Torah. The author of all five of the books is Moses, the original Moses. The titles of the books of the Torah are: Genesis, Exodus, Leviticus, Numbers, and Deuteronomy. That was the order in our Holy Book. It was the same order in the Bible sent from the sky.

In the New Testament there were four divisions: The Gospels, The Acts of the Apostles, The Letters of the Apostles to various churches and individuals, and the Revelation of Jesus Christ. There were twenty-seven books in all. I decided to first read a sampling of the New Testament books to get a feel of what was being presented.

I discovered in some preface material the Gospels covered the time from the birth of the Messiah to his death by crucifixion by some empire referred to as the Romans. I found John's Gospel to be very revealing and very disturbing. Jesus was born as one of the Chosen people, but the leaders of the Chosen did not believe he was the Messiah. Even in the face of supernatural miracles of healing, they would not believe. They seemed to ignore the fact he had even restored the life of a man who had been dead for four days. That was completely incomprehensible.

The Jews believed the Messiah would come as a king and his kingdom would return the Chosen people to a position of power after they banished the Romans. This man, this Jesus, was the son of a carpenter. He was not going to lead an army to route the Romans from the Promised Land. It turned out, the Romans may have crucified Jesus, but the Jews, the Chosen, manipulated these

Romans into nailing him to the cross. The similarities between the Gospel and what just happened in New Jerusalem with the stranger haunted me.

I scanned the other three Gospels and even though each book contained unique information, there was much overlap. The more I read, the more I began to believe the things the stranger accused us of were true. We had lost our compassion for our fellow man.

I prayed on this and fasted for several days. My soul was tormented by my memories of what I had almost done to him. I became so distraught, I could not sleep and began walking in my chambers every night, sometimes prostrating on my balcony begging God to forgive me for my sins, for there were many … so very many sins.

One night, while I lay on my balcony, recounting my sins, the beam appeared again. It illuminated me in a blue white light and I looked up and saw something was descending. I couldn't make it out, but I moved out of the light, afraid this might be my judgment day. I prepared to be punished. It turned out to be a large box covered in the light blue fabric that had covered the Holy Bible. I discovered it was on rollers and I could easily move it off the balcony into my chambers. I carefully unwrapped the box and stored the blue fabric along with the other wrapping in a storage closet. The box was easy to open and the first thing I noticed was a letter that had writing on the outside: "To the Moses, Please open this first."

I sat at my desk and opened the envelope with fear and trepidation. The letter read as follows:

To the Moses at New Jerusalem,

109

Greetings from the Stranger and Servant Anna. My real name is Hiroshi Koyama and Anna is no longer a servant, she is now my wife. We were just married.

We are orbiting the Earth in a spaceship and pass over New Jerusalem every 90 minutes. Our ship is a Generation Ship named *Hope.*

We hope you received the Holy Bible we sent to you, and have taken time from your busy schedule to begin reading it. I requested it be sent to you from our chaplain. He is the religious leader on our ship.

Before I beamed down to visit New Jerusalem, we attempted to communicate with you numerous times. Unfortunately, we were not successful, and I was sent as an envoy to begin discussions. That did not work out well either. We are still very interested in opening a dialog with you. That is why we sent you this box. It contains a communication system that will allow us to see and speak to each other without fear of arrest or attack.

We are sure Security Priest Simon, or other SPs, will assume the vid com system is a bomb or a device to steal information as a precursor to our attack. I assure you it is not. Please have your computer people check out the vid com system before the SPs attempt to destroy it.

The shipping box also contains an instruction manual to assist your computer people in setting it up. Once it is up and running, it will automatically send us a message. At that time, we will attempt to contact you.

All of us aboard *Hope* look forward to beginning peaceful discussions.

I read through the letter two additional times. I felt encouraged by the words, but couldn't help fear this might be a setup for some type of disaster. After praying for guidance on this matter, I felt very tired. I hadn't slept for several days. I decided I really needed to be well rested before making any decisions.

I retired to my bed chambers, dimmed the lights and laid down on my bed. I believe I fell asleep the second my head touched the pillow.

Security Priest Simon

"What do you mean the Moses won't see me? I've had this meeting scheduled for over a week." I was becoming very annoyed with the Moses' chief aide.

He responded back to me in a calm, but firm voice. "The Moses gave very specific instructions, he is not to be disturbed until he notifies me."

"How long has it been since you last had contact with him?"

"Three days, SP."

"Three days!" I shouted at the aide. "He could be sick or had an accident. Someone should…"

"The Moses is fine, SP. We continually monitor his vital signs and…" he paused to look at the output from the medical monitors, "at the moment, he is sleeping. Praise God for that. He hasn't slept for two days. He needs his rest. I will contact you as soon as he is awake. Can I help you with anything else?"

I shook my head angrily at the aide, turned on my heels and left the lobby of the Moses' offices. By the time I walked to my office on the other side of the Temple, I'd calmed down some. I sat in my chair, closed my eyes and tried to breathe deeply, but I still hurt all over from the beating the stranger gave me less than a week ago. If I took too deep a breath, the cracked ribs really pained me. So help me, if I ever see that brown-eyed bastard again, he's a dead man.

One of my junior security priests stuck his head in the door and said, "Hey boss, got a minute?"

I nodded and said, "Thirty seconds, and it better be important." My head began to throb and I made a mental note not to move my head again soon.

"We got a report from one of the protectors on night shift that he saw a blue-white light beam last night, around two am."

My eyes snapped open. "Exactly, what did he say?"

He shrugged his shoulders as he thought for a moment then said, "He was on foot patrol close to Ring Gate 3 North when he saw a beam of light shine down from the bottom of a cloud."

"Did he say where the light beam touched down?"

The SP shook his head. "I asked him and he said he really couldn't tell. There were a lot of buildings in the way, but somewhere close to the Temple."

I started to standup quickly, but the pain was too intense and I settled back into my chair. I yelled, "I want to see that protector right now! You hear me? Right now!"

Quartermaster Geoffrey Taylor

"Governor, captain, we're here this morning to present the recommendations of the Shuttle Committee. We're recommending five of the ship's shuttles be used to evaluate a total of ten of the American National Lab sites. Each shuttle will visit two labs located relatively close together. The labs were selected based on the likelihood they could provide the materials needed by *Hope* to sustain and repair our ship. We recommend a crew of at least four be used to operate each shuttle, which would include two pilots and two security personnel. We believe a seven day mission would be sufficient to do a preliminary investigation of both locations for each shuttle. Follow-up missions could be authorized only if these first explorations warrant a closer inspection. Are there any questions at this point?"

The governor nodded towards the captain. Captain Lawrence said, "The governor and I both like the plan. Two questions: one, do you have recommendations for the crew assignments, and two, when would the shuttles leave?"

"Addressing question one," I said, "Yes, we do have recommendations of the crew assignments and two, all five shuttles can depart hours after your approvals."

I put up a table on the view screen showing which shuttles would visit which labs and crew assignments:

Shuttle Alpha – Lawrence Livermore and Lawrence Berkeley

Shuttle Bravo—Los Alamos and Sandia

Shuttle Charlie—Argonne and Fermi

Shuttle Delta—Morgantown and Pittsburg

Shuttle Echo— Princeton and Brookhaven

The governor snorted at the mission for Shuttle Alpha. "Captain, are the two labs in old California named after relatives of yours?"

The captain replied, "Of course, the Lawrence families have been a force in the science communities for centuries. Perhaps I should volunteer for pilot in command so I can see the old homestead. But I suppose I should let the younger generation handle this trip.

"Governor, if you agree, I think this plan is spot on and as far as I'm concerned, the mission is a go."

The governor nodded in agreement and said, "Yes, I also agree. Good work quartermaster, tell your committee we thank you all for a job well done. We look forward to seeing the results of these missions.

The Moses

I awoke from a deep sleep feeling truly refreshed for the first time in days. I noticed the red alert light blinking on the night stand next to my bed. I ignored it and headed for the bathroom. After taking care of business, I headed into my office. I wanted to have my technical people come in to help me set up the vid com system, but as I reached for the call button to speak with my aide, I heard a pounding on my doors. It startled me. Were we under attack? Was there some type of emergency? I pressed the call button and said in an annoyed voice, "What in the name of the seven hells is going on out there? Who's pounding on my doors? Contact security and have them removed at once."

The strained voice of my aide replied, "I'm so sorry, Your Holiness. It's Security Priest Simon. He demands to see you. He believes you are in great danger and he wants to make sure you are all right."

A chill ran through me, *does he know about the vid com package? That can't be possible.* "Tell that buffoon to stop pounding on my door. I'm not even dressed yet. Tell him to sit down and wait until I am ready to see him. Also mention if I hear one more disturbance outside my door, I will personally punish him with a level six stun."

The pounding stopped. I quickly looked around for a place to hide the package. I decided on my bathroom area. They were in the process of making modifications and the package would fit in nicely. I pushed it through the bathroom doors and slid it behind a carpenter's work bench where it fit in with the rest of the mess.

I returned to my bedroom and quickly changed clothes. I didn't shave or comb my hair. I wanted the SP to see that he was interrupting my morning ritual. I sat down at my desk and called my aide and told him to send the SP in. I didn't unbolt the door on purpose. I wanted him to see what a pain he was. When the door did not open, he knocked politely this time and I touched a control on my desk and the door bolts snicked open.

As he walked towards my desk he was already apologizing, "I'm so sorry for disturbing you, Your Holiness. But I was very concerned for your well being." He stood in front of my desk however I didn't invite him to sit down.

I glared at him and said in a gruff voice, "What was the reason for your concern, SP? This better be very good."

"May I sit down, Your Holiness? I have not completely recovered from the injuries I sustained in my fight with that accursed stranger."

"No you may not. You won't be here that long. Get on with what you have to say."

He grimaced and said, "Last night, one of my protectors saw a light beam that seemed to touch down somewhere on the Temple grounds. I was concerned the stranger or worse, several of his companions, had come to do you harm."

I glared up at him. "Do I appear to be suffering from any harm? Do you want to search my quarters to make sure boogey men aren't hiding under my bed?"

He answered in a meek voice, "Your Holiness, it is my sworn duty to make sure you are not in any danger. Would you allow me five minutes to do a quick search of your rooms?"

I nodded. "I'll give you two minutes. Make it quick." He turned back towards the open doors and gestured to two of his protectors to begin the search. I slammed my hand down on my desk top and said, "Just you SP. I don't want your men pawing through my things."

He started at the balcony and made a quick sweep of the office, then moved to my bedroom. He actually looked under my bed, then moved towards the bathroom. He opened the doors and stood in the entry way and did a quick sweep with his eyes. I held my breath, but with all the construction clutter, I doubt if he noticed the package.

He came back to my desk and bowed low. "Thank you for allowing me to do my duty Your Holiness. I won't bother you any further."

He turned quickly and left my office, closing the door behind him. I let out a long breath and tried to relax. I commed my aide and said, "Has he left?"

"Yes Your Grace, he's gone."

"I'll have breakfast in my office this morning. Oh, by the way, I'm having some problems with my computer. Please have a tech visit me after I've eaten."

Captain David Lawrence

I looked at the vid screen displaying the status of the five shuttles. All five had been launched. Their launches had been staggered based on the distance to their respective targets. *Hope's* orbit was from west to east. As we approached the west coast of North America, Shuttle Alpha was the first to launch. The two Lawrence Labs were located near the ruins of San Francisco. As our orbit traveled eastward across the continent, shuttles were launched when we neared their assigned labs. The last to launch was Shuttle Echo. Their target labs were both close to the east coast.

All the shuttles were tasked with making high altitude flyovers to visually assess the status of the lab areas. Attempts to communicate with the labs would be made. The next step was low-level, high speed runs from several directions over the target area. Vids and audio records were made of all runs. We were looking for some signs of civilization. We were also checking on the possibility of hostile scavenger presence. All this information would be transmitted back to *Hope* for analysis. If anything looked promising, and no hostile contact was made, low-level, low speed runs were authorized. Landings and personal contact were authorized only when we were sure the lab had something to offer us in the way of resupply and retrofits.

We didn't expect any reports from the shuttles for at least a day after launch. We were surprised to hear from Shuttle Alpha eleven hours later.

"*Hope,* this is Shuttle Alpha, over."

"Shuttle Alpha, this is *Hope,* go ahead, over."

"No joy on our targets. The whole area is underwater. Both labs are flooded. Estimate they are covered by at least fifty feet of sea water. Awaiting instructions. Over."

"Shuttle Alpha, return to *Hope.* Rendezvous at time and coordinates sent to your nav com. Confirm, over."

"Roger *Hope,* confirm Shuttle Alpha to return to *Hope* at time and coordinates sent to nav com. Shuttle Alpha, over and out."

The Moses

The red light on my desk flashed. My aide said, "Your Holiness, the computer tech you requested is here."

"Wait ten minutes and send him in."

"Understood, Your Holiness."

I closed the Holy Bible on my desk and got up and walked to the bathroom. I pushed the package out to my office, removed the components and set them on a side table along with the instruction manual. I briefly skimmed through the manual to see if anything indicated it was from a space ship. There were none, but I was surprised to see a reference to Oak Ridge National Lab. That named sounded familiar.

There was a knock on my door and I said in a loud voice, "Enter."

I returned the manual to the table with the vid com components and turned to meet the computer tech. He was a good looking young man, close-cut blond hair, blue eyes (of course), wearing dark blue coveralls with the words Dr. John

Sanborn, Computer Tech written on his ID badge next to his star. He was one of the Chosen.

He stopped in front of my desk, in a stance that almost resembled a military posture and said in a pleasant voice, "Good morning, Your Holiness. I'm John Sanborn. I understand you are having a problem with your computer?"

I gestured for him to sit down and I also sat and said, "Actually, Dr. Sanborn, I received a new vid com system from the ancient's lab and I would greatly appreciate it if you could put it together, get it running and show me how to operate it. Do you think you can do that?"

He looked over at the table with the various components displayed. "I believe so, Your Holiness. May I look at the parts?" I gestured to the table and he got up and walked over and began examining the components. I watched him and noticed a smile forming upon his face. He turned to me and said, "I'm positive I can put this together, but I'm not sure how you will be able to use it. In order to communicate with someone, they have to have a similar system. To the best of my knowledge, these don't exist anymore. You said it was from the ancient's lab?"

I gestured for him to sit back down. "Dr Sanborn, as one of the Chosen, you have a security clearance, is that correct?"

"Yes, Your Holiness. I have a Top Secret clearance due to the nature of my work."

"Excellent. This vid com system was discovered recently in a previously unexplored portion of the lab. There were several other systems also discovered, all in boxes and presumably not assembled. One was previously assembled, possibly by the ancients themselves. It appears in working order, but we need this one to be assembled to test their viability as an improvement to our communication network. I order you to tell no one about this, not even your director or any SP. If you are successful in getting this system operational, you will be promoted to become the new director of your organization, but you cannot tell anyone. If you do, your punishment will be … life threatening. Do you understand me?"

He began to speak, but had to clear his throat. He coughed, then said, "Yes, Your Holiness, I understand perfectly."

"Excellent. Tell me Dr. Sanborn, are you married?"

He shook his head.

"Then you will remain in this office until the system is assembled and tested. There is a guest bathroom adjacent to my office. It has a shower. You will take your meals here and a cot will be brought in for you to sleep on. How long do you think it will take you to assemble the system and have it tested?"

"No more than two days, barring anything unforeseen occurring."

"Do you have a personal com device? If so you need to surrender it to me now." The confused tech reached into his breast pocket, took out his com cell and handed it to me. "I'll contact your boss and let him know you are on a special assignment for me and will not be returning until it is completed. Have you eaten lunch?"

He shook his head. I pushed the call button on my desk and my aide responded. I made the necessary arrangements, then I also ordered him that none of this information was to be shared with anyone else, especially not Senior Priest Simon. I closed by warning him that if any of this information was leaked to anyone, everyone on my staff would be punished and replaced.

I could hear an audible gulp followed by, "Understood perfectly, Your Holiness. What would you like for lunch?"

Captain David Lawrence

"So far, governor, we're zero for three on the other labs," I said. "It doesn't look promising. The labs on the west coast were under water, *way* under water. The two in the southwest desert were buried in sand. Shuttle Bravo had exact coordinates and didn't see anything but sand, sagebrush, and cactus. No radio contact of any kind. Shuttle Charlie had similar results to Alpha. The whole area is flooded. The labs were both close to Lake Michigan and the old city of Chicago. The only thing they could identify was the top of the John Hancock Building."

The governor clenched his jaw. "How does the crew know about the John Hancock Building? Your pilots were born on *Hope,* just like the rest of us. Was somebody a history buff?"

"Apparently so," I answered. "When Flight Control asked how he knew it was the John Hancock Building, the pilot told him it was just like the picture in a book his great-great-grandfather kept."

"What's the status on the last two shuttles?" the governor asked.

I answered, "Delta is due to report in twelve hours, Echo, a couple of hours later."

"Thanks for the update, captain. Please keep me informed."

LCDR Hiroshi Koyama

We were in an electric cart traveling on a road in the inside-out world. It was Anna's first tour and she was like a little kid with a new toy. Her experiences of being outside were limited to the wastelands surrounding New Jerusalem. On *Hope,* outside was spectacular. There were all type of trees, tall green trees growing high towards the centerline of the barrel. There were dozens of orchards of different types of fruit trees; tall pine, fir, and spruce trees grown for the lumber they would provide. Acres and acres of various vegetables and grains were also growing. Interspersed amongst the crops were ranges of grass to serve as feed for cattle, sheep, goats, and horses. Horses were used to pull plows, wagons and harvesting equipment.

We stopped at a roadside restaurant to have lunch. It was one of my favorite spots to eat when I was out on patrol duty. I was on three days leave for our honeymoon and I wanted to take Anna to show her what life was like here.

I ordered for us: bacon cheeseburgers with fries and ice cold beer brewed at our local brewery. Anna loved it. Everything tasted so good. It was Anna's first beer. She took a big gulp and swirled it around in her mouth before swallowing. She had a big smile on her face as she said, "Not brash or obtuse, just delicious." I agreed. It was a nice change from eating in the mess hall.

The mess hall food was okay, it had some other positive features as well. Anna would have breakfast there two or three times a week. She was making lots of friends among the crew. She liked talking with them over breakfast. And there was such a big variety of dishes for her to sample.

122

We were debating about splitting a piece of apple pie when my com unit chimed. The Moses made contact! We ordered the pie to go and hurried back to our Communication Center. The automatic reply was flashing on the screen when we entered the Com Center I stepped in front of the camera and nodded to the tech to open the channel. A red light went on over the screen as the tech pointed at me.

"This is the stranger. Is the Moses available to speak with me?"

I waited for several minutes. The image of a young man with blond hair and blue eyes was staring back at me. He looked startled, but said, "Hello, I'm computer tech Dr. John Sanborn. I'm here with the Moses. We have just finished putting the vid com system together and this is our first communication. To whom am I speaking?"

I wasn't sure what to say, I was expecting to see the Moses and not a tech. Before I could speak, I heard the Moses' voice say, "Thank you John. I'll take it from here. I need complete privacy for this call. Please go to the lobby and remain there until I summon you." The man turned and bowed slightly to someone off camera and stepped away.

The Moses stepped into view and looked at me. I was dressed in my uniform and must have looked very different from the last time we met. I spoke first, "Hello Your Grace, It's nice to see you again. You can call me Hiroshi Koyama

"It is much nicer to meet you under these circumstances, Mr. Koyama. Thank you for your gifts. The Holy Bible has been a blessing. Is the servant girl still with you?"

"Yes my wife is right here." If that information surprised him, he didn't show it.

123

I motioned for Anna to join me and she stepped next to me. "Hello Your Holiness. It's nice to see you again."

He smiled and replied, "So I see congratulations are in order. Did you have a church wedding?"

"Not exactly. The church wasn't big enough so we were married in a very big room with several hundred people. The man who married us is called a chaplain, similar to a minister or a priest. He read from a copy of the same Bible Hiroshi sent you when we left New Jerusalem. I believe it was a proper church wedding without the church."

His smile got even bigger and he nodded his head and said, "Would you mind if I offered my own blessing to your marriage?"

Anna looked at me and we both nodded and turned back to the Moses. I said, "We would be honored to have your blessing."

We bowed our heads as the Moses said, "Our heavenly Father, please bless these two young people as they begin their lives together. Watch over them and protect them. Keep them safely in the hollow of your hands. Amen."

"Thank you. That means very much to both of us," said Anna.

She continued to stand beside me as I said to the Moses. "Before we begin any serious discussion, I would like to recommend that you watch a short vid that explains where we are now. It takes about twenty minutes to watch. It's called *The Generation Ship Hope.* All you have to do is say to the screen, 'Computer, play Generation Ship Hope vid.'"

We signed off. Thirty minutes later a chime sounded for an incoming com. I said to the screen, "Accept com." Once again, the Moses was looking at us from the screen. "That certainly explains a lot. Are you on the *Hope* ship now?"

"Yes sir, we are in orbit miles above you."

He was silent for a minute and then said, "I need to consider all of this and I have other commitments to take care of. Would it be possible to reach you tomorrow at this time?"

"Of course."

"Thank you. We'll speak more tomorrow. Good night, and again, congratulations on your marriage."

Captain David Lawrence

I was sitting in my office going over the reports from the first three shuttles when the call came in. "Captain, this is the XO. I'm in Flight Control and we have an emergency."

"On my way," I replied as I dropped everything and headed for the Flight Control office. I arrived to a room with many concerned faces. "Give me a sit-rep, XO," I ordered.

"Cap, Shuttle Delta declared an emergency. They are under attack. They have identified the attackers as two old F-35 aircraft."

"What!?" I sputtered. "That can't be correct. That model of aircraft was mothballed before we left Earth. What's the status of Delta?"

"We believe they were shot down, sir."

My knees buckled, but only slightly. "Do we have a vid com of the attack?"

"Yes sir."

"Play it."

A four-view, split screen display showed up on the vid. One showed a front view from the shuttle, one a rear view, one was a moving map display of their location, and the last was a display of their instruments. The pilot was in the middle of reporting his position. "…Roger, *Hope* this is Delta. In route to mother, ETA forty-five minutes. Current position, low and slow over…I think those are troops? …Yes, confirm troop movement heading south. Counting ten, fifteen, eighteen large troop transports on ground. Are those tanks, Hawk? Yes, Hawk confirms five tanks … artillery—"

At that point the computer voice came on: "Warning, attack imminent, Warning, attack imminent. Warning—"

The voice of Hawk, the co-pilot, was talking over the warning, "Missile lock cap, break right, break right, now … Incoming!!!"

The pilot said, "Full power now. Climbing to orbi…"

The vid screen changed abruptly to static. They were gone.

Everyone in the room was silent, staring at me, waiting for orders. "Give me a rear view replay from the moment of missile lock. Full screen."

This rear recording showed some type of vehicle pursuing the shuttle. It was so far away, the craft could not be identified. "Pause and magnify image ten times, center the pursuit craft."

A crystal clear image of a Navy F-35B Lightning II aircraft was displayed. Also pictured was a missile that had just been launched from its internal weapons bay. To the rear, and to the starboard side, a second F-35B could be seen.

"I confirm two F-35B attack aircrafts."

The XO said, "I thought the Navy used the C model."

I replied, "They did. The Marines used the B model."

"How can you tell the difference?"

"The B model has no tail hook. They have VTOL capability."

"What's VTOL?"

"It stands for Vertical Take Off and Landing. That's why they don't have tail hooks."

"How do you know all that about an ancient airplane?" asked the XO incredulously.

"I had a distant relative who was a Marine pilot. He flew the F-35B. I've got an old picture of him somewhere. It's just useless trivia. What's the status of Echo?" I asked, changing the subject.

"Echo is currently in route to *Hope.* Altitude, thirty thousand feet. Speed, one-point-five mach."

"XO, have them reroute Echo to attack site. Climb to and maintain fifty thousand feet. Loiter speed. I want recon pictures of everything." I paused then added, "Have them check for survivors."

As I turned to leave, everyone snapped to attention and saluted. I stopped, also came to attention, returned their salutes and said, "Carry on."

The Moses

I sat at my desk, deep in thought. I dismissed Dr. Sanborn after first admonishing him to not speak of his activities in my office to anyone. I reminded him of the consequences if he violated my order. Next, I told him to expect his promotion within the week. As my predecessor taught me, first threaten the stick, then mention the honey. That advice has served me well during my reign.

My mind was reeling from information overload. Where to begin? I decided on the vid of the ship *Hope.* What an incredible undertaking. A two hundred year mission seemed like a fantasy concocted by a child. But the details of the vid seemed so real. The interviews with the original crew, the tours of the ship, pictures of the ship's assembly in orbit, high above the Earth, all these details lent credence to the story. But what if it was all a lie? What would they hope to gain? I answered my own question; the conquest of New Jerusalem and access to the ancient's lab.

The one point I couldn't dispute was the beam. Hiroshi and Anna escaped death by stoning by riding the beam into the sky; the delivery of the Holy Bible, also from the sky. Finally, the delivery of the vid com system and the conversation with Hiroshi and Anna; that had to be real. Why did I still feel unsure? After a few minutes of musing, a solution occurred to me.

I went to the vid com and hailed Hiroshi. Within five minutes, his image appeared on the screen. I offered my proposal. "Hiroshi, the vid of the ship was most impressive, but I must be sure. I must not have any doubts of the genuineness of what I saw. The only way I can feel comfortable moving forward is for me to visit *Hope*. Is that something you'd be willing to arrange?"

Hiroshi looked surprised, but then was nodding his head in agreement. "Would you like a tour of the ship?"

"Absolutely, but I can only afford to be gone for an hour. And one more thing, I would like Senior Security Priest Simon to accompany me. I can't do this in a vacuum."

A slow smile spread across Hiroshi's face. He said, "Yes, I see the need for you to do that. I take it the SP has been promoted?"

"Yes, just recently, he's the head of my security."

Hiroshi nodded and continued to smile. "I need to get the approval from my captain and the ship's governor, but I think we will be able to accommodate your request. When would you like to take your tour?"

"I need to speak with the SSP first. May I get back to you in an hour?" I asked. "Is that acceptable?"

"That would give me time to talk with my commanding officer and the governor. Speak to you in an hour."

We broke contact and I picked up my com unit and commed SP Simon, soon to become the SSP.

"Yes, Your Holiness. How may I me be of service?"

"I need you in my office as soon as you can get here." I broke contact without any further information.

Ten minutes later, there was a knock on my door. "Enter." I rose to welcome the SP. His face was red and he was breathing heavily as he stood before my desk.

"Sit down, SP. Thank you for being so prompt. Would you like a glass of water?" He nodded his head and mumbled his thanks. After his drink, he started to take a deep breath, but thought better of it as he seemed to feel a pain in his side. I sat down and faced him, a smile on my face, attempting to look friendly. "I called you here for three reasons. The first one is to apologize for being so gruff with you. After all, you were only doing your job. And, in reviewing your performance during the last year, I noticed you have done your job very well. Therefore, I've decided to promote you to Senior Security Priest. All of the Security Priests will now report directly to you. You will be moving into a new, larger office next to mine."

He had been taking another sip of water, but when he heard the news he began to cough and choke. I got up and moved behind him and patted him on the back. He looked at me with an admiration I had never seen previously. "Thank you, Your Holiness. This means so much to me. I will be in your debt for as long as I live."

I smiled and returned to my seat. "Now, for the second reason I sent for you. I have a confession to make. When the stranger and the servant girl escaped the stoning pit, they apparently floated up to heaven on a sunbeam."

The SP was up and out of his chair in a heartbeat. "Surely, Your Holiness you can't believe …"

I raised my hand for silence, and he reluctantly returned to his seat. "It's best if you let me finish, then you can ask me questions. At the time, I had no idea where they went. But later, late in the evening, that same light beam showed up on my balcony and a package traveled down the beam and deposited itself on the balcony floor."

I could tell he wanted to refute what I was saying, but he remained quiet. "The package turned out to be a Holy Bible, not the deteriorating fragments like we have, but a complete intact Bible. Let me show it to you."

I stood and motioned him to follow. There, on the table next to the case where our remnants of the Old Testament were displayed, was the Bible sent down from the ship. He looked at it as if it were a snake ready to strike. "It's a fake. It has to be. It's a work of Satan, the great deceiver. Surely, you don't believe this is…"

"Please stop protesting. Open the cover and read the inscriptions. There are two. Please read them both."

He began to reading, but I stopped him, "Out loud please."

"It says, 'To the crew of the Generation Ship *Hope,* May Captain Noah guide his Ark to a new Promised Land. May God sail with you and guide your way.'"

"Do you notice the date? That dedication was written over two hundred years ago."

"It's a lie. How can a two hundred year old book be in such pristine condition?" I didn't answer, instead I ordered him to read the second dedication. "To the Moses of New Jerusalem, May you find the truth. The truth will set you free."

"Did you notice the date, SP? It was dedicated the day after the stranger and the servant girl rode the beam into the sky."

"No, it cannot be. It's not possible. It goes against everything we have ever learned. It cannot…"

"Silence!!!" I shouted as I slammed my hand down on the table next to the Bible. "Am I not the religious authority in New Jerusalem?"

"Of course, Your Holiness, I did not mean to challenge…"

I interrupted him. "I've spent the last week going through the Bible that came from the sky and, after a very thorough examination, I have concluded it is completely true. Nowhere does it differ from our Bible. It is, in fact, superior to our Bible because it is complete; not portions, not scraps, but a totally complete Bible. It was sent from a ship that is in orbit around the Earth. That ship is called *Hope.* That is where the stranger and the servant girl went when they rode the beam into the clouds. By the way, the stranger's name is Hiroshi."

The SP's head snapped up and he challenged me, "How can you possibly know that?"

"His full name is Hiroshi Koyama. He is an officer aboard the orbiting ship."

The SSP's mouth dropped open in amazement. "You've been in contact with him, haven't you? He's here, isn't he? He rode that cursed light beam down to your balcony and he's hiding here. He's in these very quarters. You're consorting with a heretic, the man you condemned to be stoned to death. How could you!!!?" he screamed at me.

I slapped him hard across the face. "How dare you condemn me? Who do you think you are to insult the Moses?"

The force of my slap knocked him back in his chair and he put his hand to his face. He recognized his mistake and immediately looked down at the floor. He slid to the floor and kneeled in front of me, and said, "I'm so sorry, Your Grace. Please forgive me. It is out of concern for your welfare that I said those things that man is…"

"Quiet," I said, more subdued. "You don't know him either, but you will. You also are assuming I'm a dupe and haven't considered this as a ruse. Which leads to the third reason I ordered you here. You and I are going to visit the orbiting ship and meet others from the ship. We're going to discover for ourselves if they are friends or foes. First, you're going to watch a vid about the ship. I assure, you the stranger is not here. But he did send me a vid com that permits us to communicate. Come with me now. We will watch it together."

LCDR Hiroshi Koyama

I contacted both the captain and the governor to ask permission for the Moses and his security chief to visit the ship for a short tour. I was shocked to hear Shuttle Delta had been shot down. "Should I postpone their visit?" I asked.

The captain said, "I'd like to go ahead and schedule it for tomorrow. We may have some intel on where the the troops are heading. That target could possibly be New Jerusalem. It would be a chance for us to give them a warning about a possible invasion. What do you think governor?"

"Do you think we will be able to determine the potential target by tomorrow? I'd hate to have them prepare for a war and then have to say we were wrong. Maybe it would be better not to mention the troop movement until we have an eighty percent certainty New Jerusalem is the target," replied the governor.

I suggested, "How about we schedule the tour for mid afternoon tomorrow and make a decision at noon whether to mention the troops or not? That gives us almost a day to make an assessment." The captain and the governor both agreed.

At precisely one hour after my last vid com with the Moses, I contacted him again. I was surprised to see Senior Security Priest Simon standing next to the Moses.

"Hello again, Your Holiness. Nice to see you again SSP Simon. Congratulations on your promotion." The SSP nodded his head in acknowledgement but did not speak. *Just as well,* I thought to myself. "Could I ask what time it is in New Jerusalem now?"

The Moses looked at his chrono and said, "It's now precisely two-fifteen in the afternoon. Why do you ask?"

"I want to compare your time with the ship's time. The time on the ship is 1530 hours. Would two-fifteen pm your time tomorrow be convenient for us to beam you to the ship?"

The Moses said, "Yes, this time tomorrow is fine. Any special instructions regarding the beam?"

"Yes. We are going to send two jumpsuits for you to wear," I answered. "One size fits all. When the beam touches the floor of your balcony, just step into the light and stand still. You'll feel no sense of motion at all and it's impossible to fall. You can breathe normally even when you're in space. The beam provides its own air. When you reach the ship, you will go through an open hatch into the ship. Just step out of the beam onto the platform. We'll be there to welcome you aboard. Any other questions?"

There were none.

Senior Security Priest (SSP) Simon

I checked my chrono, five minutes later than the last time I looked. I was nervous, perhaps somewhat frightened. Even though the jumpsuits fit well enough, I was uncomfortable wearing one. The Moses seemed completely at ease wearing his, but he shouldn't be wearing clothes sent by our enemy. He should be dressed in his Holy robes.

I've never enjoyed being in high places. The balcony of the Temple was only three stories above the ground, but I could tell my heart rate was elevating. The Moses was standing next to me looking calm and collected, and very much in charge. I tried not to think about the journey we were about to take. If being on the balcony was frightening, I feared riding a beam into space would be terrifying. I tried taking a deep breath to calm myself, forgetting about my cracked ribs until they made themselves known with a sharp stab of pain in my side.

The last two days made no sense to me at all. It appeared the Moses was collaborating with the spawn of Satan, and yet now he seemed to be looking forward to meeting them. We were about to meet up with a man who, by all rights, should have been stoned to death for heresy. The same man who beat me so severely a week ago, I still felt the pain. And it appeared the Moses wanted us to act like they were a few of our Chosen friends.

134

The vid we watched couldn't be true. A ship that had sailed to the stars and returned two hundred years later; pure rubbish. This is a plot to kill us, to eliminate the city's religious and security leaders so our enemy will be able to easily capture New Jerusalem. I felt powerless to stop them. The Moses has been deluded by their apparent technology.

My reverie was interrupted by the presence of a bright light. The sunbeam arrived at the Temple balcony. It might as well have been called a death ray. The Moses stepped into the light, but I hesitated. In a cheerful voice, he said to me, "Step into the light Simon or prepare to be stripped of all rank and banished from New Jerusalem for the rest of your life."

The Moses had such a way with words.

We started to slowly move upward. I closed my eyes tightly and waited for death. I could hear the Moses' voice very clearly. "What a glorious view. Open your eyes Simon. Isn't this incredible?" He sounded like a child with a new toy instead of someone on their way to meet death. In a more authoritarian tone, the Moses said, "Open your eyes, SSP. That is an order!"

I opened my eyes and behold, it *was* a spectacular view! There was no sense of motion at all. It was as if we were not moving; as if were New Jerusalem moving down and away from us. I could see everything in the city in great detail. As it moved further downward, I could see the lands outside the city, fields where crops were growing, animals grazing in pastures, lakes and the streams that fed them. I realized I had never seen any of this before. I was born inside the walls of New Jerusalem and never had a need to venture outside.

As we continued to rise I could see rolling hills in the distance and beyond, mountains with white tops. Could that be snow?

Surely not during this season. Suddenly, my view was obscured as we moved into a cloud. I could no longer see the ground below. I looked up and, as we exited the cloud, saw the sky a darker shade of blue. The blue continued to darken and I thought I could begin to see pin points of light. Could those be stars? They couldn't be, stars don't shine in the daytime.

I looked directly above me and saw the sunbeam heading toward a small silver … silver something. I looked down again and could no longer see New Jerusalem but I could see an ocean of water and higher mountains and so much more. Looking back up, the silver thing was rapidly growing in size. And those *were* stars! Hundreds, perhaps even thousands, of stars lying on a blanket of the darkest blackness I'd ever seen.

In a few moments the stars were obscured by a gigantic structure, I assumed it was the ship. The beam disappeared into an opening in the side of the ship. A few moments later, we were stepping off a platform into a small room with only a small group of people. They were mostly dressed in military uniforms, even the women. The only woman not in uniform I recognized as Servant Anna. She was standing next to my nemesis.

There was an awkward moment of silence, followed by a flash of light with the slight smell of ozone. A man in uniform with four gold braids on his sleeve stepped forward with his right hand extended. He said, "Good afternoon gentlemen, I'm Captain David Lawrence, welcome aboard the Generation Ship *Hope*. That bright flash you experienced was to protect you from any ship-born pathogens while you are onboard. If you will follow me, we will begin our ship tour in our conference room."

We followed the captain out of the Beam Room and headed down a hallway. There were numerous pictures hung on both walls showing groups of men and women all dressed in military uniforms. The Moses asked, "Why are all these pictures hung on the walls, captain?"

We continued to walk as the captain replied, "These are pictures of all of the ship's military officers. We take one every ten years. Our complete round trip time has been a little over two hundred years so there are twenty pictures."

We stopped briefly near a doorway next to the last picture. I noticed the captain was included along with other officers. I moved back to look at the previous picture and noted a younger version of the captain. I asked, "How long have you been captain of the *Hope?*"

"A little over twenty years. I joined the crew at the age of eighteen and moved up through the ranks before I was nominated to be captain."

I made a note to check the other pictures to see if I could spot the younger versions of the captain.

We entered the conference room and took seats around a table. I sat next to the Moses and the higher ranking officers were scattered around the rest of the table. The other lower ranks sat next to the wall. The Moses and I faced a wide curtained wall. In the back of the room was a credenza covered with water, tea, coffee, fruit juices and assorted trays of pastries. It was obvious they knew how to pamper their guests.

A large, older man dressed in civilian clothes was the last to enter and he closed the hallway door behind him. He went to the head of the table where a rostrum stood and said, "Good afternoon, I'm Governor John Stewart. I'm responsible for the civilian population on *Hope.* I've been told you've already seen the ship's introductory vid. Is that correct?"

The Moses replied, "I'm called the Moses. I'm the religious leader of New Jerusalem. As I'm sure you know, New Jerusalem is a theocratic city state. Sitting next to me is Senior Security Priest Simon. He's responsible for maintaining the peace in the city. We thank you for inviting us here. We both feel we have learned a tremendous amount from your vid, but our real questions are focused on why you've chosen to interact with New Jerusalem."

The governor nodded and said, "We will definitely cover that in a few minutes, but first I would like to briefly address another issue. We want to prove to you, as best we can, that we are not a threat to you. *Hope* is not a warship. It has no offensive weapons at all and only limited defensive capabilities. Our mission was to explore a distant star and determine if it had a planet orbiting that star where human beings could survive. We found the planet, it's called Proxima B and many men, women and children chose to leave the ship and establish a colony there. The rest of *Hope's* population returned to Earth to share all the information gained in our travels. As the vid showed, we are a generation ship. The original crew that left Earth passed on long before we reached the star. In fact, another generation was born, lived their lives and also passed away before we reached the star. It was the third generation that finally attained our goal. It took another three generations to return to Earth. I want to show you how we accomplished that. Would you please join me at the window?"

The Moses and I stood and walked to the curtained wall. The curtain parted revealing a glass ceiling-to-floor window. Beyond the window was something I couldn't originally fathom. The Moses said it best, "My God, it's a complete new world contained inside the ship."

138

I was dumbfounded and barely heard the governor continue, "*Hope* is a closed system. For six generations we've grown all our own food, made our own clothes, and repaired the ship when needed. We have our own villages with hospitals and schools. But we have reached our design life. If we don't get help, *Hope* will not survive another year. That's why we've come to you. When *Hope* was built, it was so large it couldn't be built on Earth. It was built in orbit. We had a national laboratory that became responsible for shipping everything we needed to build and outfit the ship. That lab was called Oak Ridge National Laboratory. Our mission plan was that we were to return to Oak Ridge where we would be repaired, replenished, and repopulated to be sent out on another mission to another star.

The lab you call the ancient's lab is our Oak Ridge National Lab. That's why we're here. We attempted to contact you by vid com when we made orbit, but got no response. Apparently, your com systems weren't compatible with the ship's. We knew that The Plague had decimated Earth, but we needed, still need, your help to survive."

I watched the Moses. He appeared as stunned as I felt. I turned to the governor and asked, "Excuse me governor, would it be possible to take a short break? I believe we could both use your restroom."

He answered, "Of course, the restroom is just across the hall from the door to the conference room. When you're done there, please help yourselves to drinks and pastries." He turned and said the rest of the group, "Fifteen minute break."

LCDR Hiroshi Koyama

I left the conference room and hurried to Flight Control. The XO was waiting for me with the latest information on the unidentified troops' movements. With mechanized personnel transports they were making good time by staying on what was left of the superhighways.

Shuttle Echo had returned to *Hope* last night. Fortuately she had deployed spy drones to keep a continuous watch on all parts of the army. They discovered an armored command vehicle in the middle of their tanks. The tanks were Abrams M1 A4-Mod 7, very tricked out with the 150mm rapid fire cannon, rocket and mortar launchers and three fifty caliber, computer controlled, machine guns. It appeared the mechanized equipment was recovered from armories as the army moved south. It was assumed the two F-35B Lightning II were taken from two separate Navy museums along the coast.

There were four unanswered questions regarding the two F-35B aircraft. First, we needed to determine where they were currently located. We assumed they had to be close to a source of jet fuel. Weapons were an issue. It seemed unlikely live missiles would be stored near the museums where the aircraft were taken from. You just don't store live weapons close to where civilians are checking out old jet planes. Lastly, and most importantly, where would they find pilots that could fly the most sophisticated fighter aircraft ever built?

Fortunately the Echo pilot was still in the Flight Control office and I asked him those four questions. He said the F-35B has vertical takeoff and landing capabilities so they could be bases almost anywhere. But they needed to refuel, which meant they were probably hanging around existing fuel depots on a Navy or Coast Guard base. Missiles probably came from weapons storage facilities again on a Navy base. According to the Echo shuttle pilot, finding a driver for the F-35B was a no brainer. The pilot said, "The voice controlled autopilot system on that aircraft is so sophisticated, any pilot who has access to the F-35 Fighter Combat Vid Game can figure it out pretty quickly. You don't have to fly the plane, you just tell it where to go and what to do."

The best news was, he knew likely places the planes might be based. Apparently, many pilots are flight junkies. They have all the specs on every fighter aircraft ever made all the way back to the Wright Flyers, Jennys, Nieuports, Spads, Folkers, and Sopwith Camels. Whatever those were.

We had the ensign do a search on the sites the shuttle pilot considered as probable bases and fuel depots. I was surprised at how fast we found the planes.

I met quietly with the captain before the break ended and reviewed the information I'd received from Flight Control. "It doesn't look good for New Jerusalem," I said to the captain. "Our Control Center calculates a ninety percent certainty that's the bad guys' target. There's nothing else of value in that wasteland area."

The captain said, "I wish we had some way to get rid of those two F-35s. Did Flight Control find any other aircraft?"

"No sir," I answered. "The best they can tell, only the two, but I had a thought about how to eliminate them. I'm sure you remember when *Hope* was being outfitted, the beam was used to bring all kinds of stuff up to the orbital construction site. I checked with the techs in the Beam Room and they said they routinely lifted equipment weighing as much as the specs of the F-35 fully loaded. Why don't we use our beam to lift each one from their respective fuel depot and drop them in the ocean?"

The captain looked at me with a blank stare and then broke into a wide grin. "Lieutenant Commander, you just earned your pay for the day. Make it happen and get vid data to show everyone. This is outstanding!!"

I ran back to the Beam Room and gave them the coordinates for the two fuel depots. I told them Captain Lawrence approved the mission. I ran back to the conference room wondering how much an Abrams tank weighed.

The meeting had not resumed yet. There was speculation the Moses and the SSP were in deep discussion about spaceships. I pulled the captain aside and told him of our successes just as the two men from New Jerusalem returned.

The Moses

I waited for everyone to take their seats. Then I stood and addressed the attendees. "I want to thank you all for hosting us this day. We have to admit, we were not prepared to hear your message. We knew nothing of your mission, and had no knowledge of this vehicle of yours. What a magnificent ship it is. We would like to return someday and visit your world within the ship. With regard to supporting your needs to refurbish *Hope,* you have our word we will do everything within our power to accommodate your requests. However we must tell you, the ancient's lab, what you call Oak Ridge National Lab, has not been totally explored. We don't have a complete inventory of what would be available, perhaps it would be more efficient to show you what we've discovered so far and compare that to your needs. Lastly, you are all welcome to visit New Jerusalem, and I promise we will be better hosts than we were when Lieutenant Koyama first visited. We need to coordinate those visits, but I feel certain we can work out the details over the next few days. "We don't wish to overstay our welcome on our first visit. We've already stayed longer than the hour requested. We, will take our leave…"

The captain interrupted my salutation. "Your Holiness, we need to inform you of something before you leave. We ask you to stay a little longer."

I nodded my head and said, "Of course captain. What is your urgent news?"

"Yesterday, one of our shuttles was investigating another lab site just in case Oak Ridge was not going to be available to support our needs. On the shuttle's return to *Hope,* it was shot down by an old jet fighter aircraft killing the crew of four. We had another shuttle in the area and diverted it to investigate the attack. That shuttle discovered an army of soldiers, along with tanks and artillery, marching towards New Jerusalem. If they continue to advance at their current speed, they will arrive at New Jerusalem in a couple of weeks."

Senior Security Priest Simon was on his feet in an instant. "Do you have any data to confirm these claims?"

"Yes we do, SSP Simon," answered the captain. "Our shuttle deployed a number of drones to monitor the unidentified army movements. These drones can stay aloft for several days and have the capacity to track the army's movements." He turned toward the vid screen and said, "Computer, play the live feed of the army movements." The vid screen displayed a picture of eighteen large troop transports, five tanks and a number of artillery pieces, moving down an old superhighway. The SSP slowly sat down. "They're moving at about 30mph, but stop during the evening to eat and sleep. Our analysts estimate they could be outside New Jerusalem in a couple of weeks if they maintain that pace. Tell me SSP, do you have any security people or protectors working outside the New Jerusalem walls?"

"No. Our protectors and security people work inside the walls to maintain order within the city. We haven't had anyone attack us in over fifty years. We didn't think there were any sizeable external threats still in existence. Would you be able to assist us if this army attacks?"

The captain answered, "Of course we will. However, as our governor said, *Hope* is not designed for combat. We have a very limited number of weapons on the ship. Having said that, while we were on our break, Lieutenant Commander Koyama was able to locate and destroy the two fighter aircraft that took part in the shooting down of one of our shuttles." That got everyone's attention. The captain turned to Koyama and said, "Narrate the vid, will you Hiroshi?"

The lieutenant commander stood and turned toward the vid screen and said, "Computer, play destruction of F-35s." The view on the vid screen changed from the movements of the army to a shot of an aircraft sitting next to a refueling truck about a half mile from the ocean. "We decided to see if the beam operating in tractor mode would be able to damage the aircraft. One of our shuttle pilots had a pretty good idea where these planes would need to be to get refueled. We quickly scanned ten locations and discovered the two aircraft. The planes had tie-down cables securing them to the ground. First we aimed the beam light on the plane."

The picture showed a bright circle of light shining onto the plane with the fuel truck next to it. A few of the armed guards were also caught in the light. "We weren't sure if the beam had enough pulling power to lift the plane, but the beams had been used in the construction of the *Hope* so we gave it a try. At first nothing happened, but then…" He waited until the plane and truck seemed to jump off the ground. Several people gasped in surprise.

"When the tie down cables broke, it turned out the beam had enough power to lift the plane, the truck and a few of the guards. We elevated everything, moved them over the ocean, then shut off the beam and let everything sink to the bottom of the sea."

The room erupted with shouts and clapping. When it subsided I said, "You are to be congratulated on you creative approach. Hopefully, if this army does make it to New Jerusalem, you will have more tricks up your sleeve."

The captain said, "We will continue to monitor the movements of the army and give you updates by vid com. I would also like to have your SSP coordinate with Lieutenant Commander Koyama to create plans for defending New Jerusalem and how to defeat the army. That's going to require us sharing information on what weapons each of us has available. Do you see that as a problem?"

The SSP began to speak, but a quick glance from me and he closed his mouth. "No problem at all, captain. We'll provide you with information of all weapons we have in New Jerusalem and those stored in the ancient's lab. We will look forward to seeing similar information from *Hope*. Don't forget to include your weaponized version of the sunbeam." That brought a chuckle to everyone.

The governor stood and said in closing, "Your Holiness, we want to thank you for requesting this meeting and for attending with your SSP. I don't think it could have come at a better time for either of us. We look forward to working with you. I also want you to know, our first priority is to defeat this enemy that appears to be threatening New Jerusalem. *Hope* will be the second priority until this enemy is defeated. We'll be in contact with you through the vid com system. For now, we wish you a safe journey back to New Jerusalem."

Part 3

The Battle of Armageddon

LCDR Hiroshi Koyama

"**W**hat are you reading, my darling husband?" asked my wife of seventy-two hours. It had been a whirlwind of activity during those three days. And it looked like the whirlwind was going to get even more intense, "I'm reading a book called, *The Art of War* by Sun Tzu."

"Oh, I love that book. I must have read it dozens of times," said Anna with tongue in cheek. "I love the sequel too, *The Art of Loving Your New Wife.* The illustrations are so graphic. Have you read it?"

I laid the book down and reached for my wife, pulling her onto my lap and whispered into her ear, "Are you feeling neglected, love of my life?"

"Not anymore," she answered and kissed me.

I kissed her back and said, "I think things are going to get worse before they get better. The war is bad enough, but having to work with SSP Simon is going to make it a lot more difficult."

"He seemed more subdued in the meeting today, maybe he's changed his mind about you," Anna replied hopefully.

"I think the presence of the Moses is largely responsible for that. But I have a vid com follow-up in an hour. I can't wait to go one on one with him," I said with more than a little sarcasm in my voice.

"Was that why you were reading that Japanese book?"

"Actually, it's a Chinese book. Sun Tzu was a great Chinese general, really a war lord, who lived in China during the sixth century BC. It's believed he never lost a battle. His book is a classic. It's been considered a manual on how to win battles for centuries. I wonder if the SSP has even heard of it."

Anna snuggled against me and said, "After your meeting with the SSP, perhaps we could practice some of the moves suggested in his second book."

I laughed and kissed her again. "I hope it's a short meeting."

SSP Simon

I was dreading this meeting, but the Moses insisted it be held. He was going to be sitting off camera, but I knew he was going to make sure I didn't become … how did he phrase it? 'too aggressive.'

To be honest, I didn't have a clue how to conduct a war. I started off as a protector when I was eighteen. I was used to dealing with sinners, not soldiers. Sometimes sinners would try to resist or escape, but very seldom did they try to kill you.

I searched our history and read up on the battle that took place fifty years ago. What I gleaned from the reports was it was more of a large mob of scavengers who overpowered the Outer Gate protectors and began looting, not an army marching here, trying to capture the city. The scavengers had clubs and knives, bows and arrows, and the occasional lance. This approaching army had tanks and cannons and all types of guns designed for one purpose: to kill us and destroy New Jerusalem.

I had no hope the stranger from the ship had any better preparation for war than I did. We both were just glorified policemen.

The Moses informed me it was time to vid com the stranger.

"Hello, Lieutenant Commander. Do you have an update for us?" I asked in my most professional voice.

He was equally professional in his response. "Good evening, Senior Security Priest. Yes I do. The army continues to move south at the same rate. They are following the same procedure of stopping for the night and setting up camp. After observing them, I'm convinced the army is made up of very well trained and disciplined soldiers. I don't believe they are scavenger gangs. I also observed that approximately twenty percent of the soldiers are female."

I had also watched the vid com coverage of the army setting up camp. I hadn't noticed female soldiers. However, I also concluded these were well trained troops, not scavengers. One thing he had not mentioned was the number of troops. I said to him, "I concur they are well trained troops. I noticed once their camp was set up they began field stripping their weapons and cleaning them."

"Yes, I noticed that too. I also noticed these were older weapons. I didn't see any laser weapons or other advanced types, did you?"

"No, I didn't see any either. I do know that we have several hundred L-300 rifles in the ancient's lab. They're the two thousand watt models. Did you notice any smart ammunition?"

"No," he replied. "Just the dumb subsonic rounds."

I changed topics. "I've attempted to get a head count of the soldiers. It looks to me there are a lot less than ten thousand. Maybe just half that many."

"I'm beginning to think you're right," Hiroshi answered. "I think the headcount was an estimate based on the capacity of the troop carriers, but if they are only half-full that makes sense. However, five thousand trained troops is still a substantial army. Are you familiar with the book, *The Art of War?*"

"By Sun Tzu? Yes, of course. I refer to it often. It's required reading for all new protectors."

Hiroshi paused, probably thinking I had never heard of Sun Tzu. "Excellent, I also read it frequently," he said. "I came across a passage today that I think applies to our situation: 'Know your enemies as well as you know yourselves and you will never lose a battle.' We know next to nothing of our enemy. According to Sun Tzu, that does not bode well for us. We need more information about who they are and why they want to invade New Jerusalem."

"I agree completely," I responded. "I'd dearly love to get my hands on a few of them for interrogation."

"What if I could get you a handful, tonight? Delivered on your door step, one at a time?"

"But how could you possibly … Oh, the beam! I love it! An excellent idea! When can I expect you to start delivery?"

"Whatever works for you. Just let me know where to drop them. Would you mind if I beamed down. I'd like to watch the master interrogator at work?"

"Absolutely, my boy. I'd love to have you attend. Let say eleven pm. Give them some time to fall asleep before you snatch them. I think the Moses balcony would be an excellent destination. Try to get an officer or two if you can."

Anna

I was in our bedroom while my husband was busy with the SSP. I decided to do some of the stretching exercises Hiroshi taught me. I think this was going to be the preparation for karate training. He wanted to make sure I was flexible enough so I didn't hurt myself doing all the moves the martial arts requires.

I was dressed in my pajamas doing deep squat and holding them for a thirty count. It sounded like his meeting ended as I placed both hands on the floor between my legs and began to move into a toe touch stance when the bedroom door burst open and Hiroshi ran in, picked me up and we flew into bed.

We hit the mattress and bounced as he began kissing me, kissing me all over. He was so excited, babbling about kidnapping soldiers as he literally ripped my pajamas off. I was laughing at his wild antics but after several more kisses and shredded pajamas, I stopped laughing.

By the time we were done, I believe we had explored every illustration in Sun Tzu's second book. I was exhausted, but Hiroshi was still hyperactive. He jumped into the shower then put on a clean uniform and headed for the door.

"Where are you going? It's time to sleep," I said.

Over his shoulder he said, "I have to go to New Jerusalem. Don't wait up." He opened the door, but turned around and smiled at me and said, "Wham bam, thank you ma'am." Then he was gone still laughing.

I lay there alone in my bed wondering what the heck that meant.

LCDR Hiroshi Koyama

I was in the Beam Room watching over the shoulder of the tech as he moved the infrared light from one sleeping soldier to another. He stopped with the light focused on a trooper sleeping on the ground at the end of a line of other sleeping soldiers. There was a six foot separation between him and the closest soldier. "How about him?" the tech asked.

"Looks good to me," I said as I checked my chrono. It was exactly eleven in New Jerusalem. Maintaining the invisible infrared light, the tech activated the tractor function and our first pick of the evening. The soldier appeared to rise into the air at a high rate of speed. Of course, the soldier felt nothing. Even if he woke and began screaming, the other sleeping troops would never hear him. Once inside the beam it was like being in a soundproof room. All we had to do was avoid the sentries as they made their rounds around the campsite.

We elevated him high enough to avoid the trees then shifted him toward New Jerusalem. Ten minutes later he was still sleeping, lying on the Moses' balcony. Within an hour, we kidnapped two more troopers, one man and one woman, and one officer, a major who had stepped out to use the latrine. At midnight, I beamed down to watch the interrogation. SSP Simon was already on the third trooper, a man in his early thirties with corporal stripes on his sleeves. The man was wild-eyed and obviously terrified. He was totally disoriented and had no idea where he was or how he got there. He looked Slavic or perhaps Middle Eastern, but his eyes were definitely blue.

SSP Simon was conducting the interrogation, the Moses was also present watching the process, perhaps to ensure he wouldn't go to extremes in his methods. In addition, two very large and imposing protectors were assisting. The corporal was strapped into a wooden chair. His arms and legs were in restraints as the SSP began.

"My name is Simon. I will be conducting your interrogation. I will ask you questions and you will answer. If you do not answer or I think you are lying to me, you will be punished." He held up a wand so the corporal could see it. "Have you ever seen a punishment wand before?"

The man shook his head and the SSP continued, "Then I need to tell you what it can do. The wand gives you an electric shock. There are eight settings. At level one you would receive a mild shock. Let me demonstrate."

He stepped forward and laid the wand on the corporal's shoulder. There was a short popping sound and the man stiffened and cried out, more from fear than from pain. "I will ask you a series of questions. You have five seconds to answer. If you chose not to answer I will give you a level one shock. I will repeat the question and if you still refuse to answer, I will then give you a level two shock. Each time you refuse to answer the wand setting is increased. By the time I get to level six there could be permanent physical damage. At level seven, brain damage may occur. At level eight brain function stops, usually death follows within a few weeks. Do you understand?"

The man said nothing and the SSP thumbed the wand to level two and stepped forward. The man screamed, "Yes. I understand."

The SSP stepped back and asked, "What is your name?"

Immediately, the man said, "I'm called Itzaak."

"What is your last name, Itzaak?"

"I do not know my last name, only Itzaak."

"Where were you born?"

"I don't know. My earliest memories are living in a place called Maine."

"How old were you then?"

"Not sure, six, maybe seven."

"Did you live with your mother and father?"

"No. I had none of those. I lived in the ruins of a city, stole food to survive."

"When did you become a soldier?"

"Not sure, nineteen or twenty. A man came and told me to go with him and he would feed me. I went. Many like me went. They fed us. Told us we were now soldiers."

"What type of soldier are you? Do you fire cannons? Drive a tank? What do you do?"

"I'm a soldier. I carry a gun, go where officers tell me to go. Shoot when they tell me to shoot. When not fighting, I'm a cook."

"What is the name of your commanding officer?"

"I don't know his name. We Just call him leader. Anyone with a yellow bar on their shoulder can be a leader. It change's a lot. Different day, different leader."

"What is the name of the leader of your army?"

"I'm not supposed to tell."

"Tell me his name or I will shock you."

He looked straight ahead and said nothing.

The SSP thumbed the wand to a level two setting and the hum of the wand increased. He stepped forward and laid the wand on Itzaak's shoulder. This time the pop was louder, but he did not cry out.

"What is the name of the leader of your army?"

Itzaak said nothing.

The SSP thumbed the wand up a setting and touched it to Itzaak's other shoulder. The pop was much louder and this time he did cry out. His head sagged to his chest and he tried to breathe deeply. He said, "If I tell you, he will kill me."

"He can't kill you if you're in our custody. Tell me his name."

He said nothing, but he was breathing hard, almost to the point of hyperventilating. The SSP thumbed the want to level four and stepped forward.

Itzaak cried out, "Wait! I'll tell you. He calls himself Angel, but I don't think that is his name."

"Just Angel?" asked Simon.

Itzaak shook his head. "No, not just Angel. Angel of Death."

The questioning stopped. Simon motioned the two protectors to undo the straps from Itzaak's arms and legs. They escorted him to a holding cell in the basement of the Temple.

When the protectors returned they were escorting a major, the last of the prisoners. He was vigorously resisting their attempts to strap him into the chair. From the looks of the cuts and bruises on his face, he had been resisting ever since being beamed to the balcony.

SSP Simon walked up behind the major and touched his shoulder with the wand. There was a loud pop which indicated at least a level three stun, maybe more. The major immediately went limp and the protectors quickly finished strapping him into the chair. One of the protectors threw a small bucket of water into the major's face and he began sputtering and regained consciousness.

SSP Simon stood in front of him and waited until he raised his head. When he did, the SSP said, "Major, I'm Senior Security Priest Simon. I will be asking you some questions. Do you understand me?"

The major raised his head and smiled at the SSP, his eyes were a bright blue. "Yes, I understand. I know exactly who you are. In fact, I know all of you. That's your religious leader you call the Moses over there. The man standing in the shadows is Lieutenant

Commander Hiroshi Koyama from the Generation Ship *Hope. Konban wah, Koyama san,"* he finished in Japanese.

"I was sent to you as a messenger and will answer all your questions, but first I will pass along the demands of the Angel, the Commanding Officer of a Generation ship you knew as *Faith. Faith* has been recommissioned. Its new name is, *The Avenging Angel.* The Angel's demands are as follows: All personnel from the *Hope* will abandon the ship and relocate to New Jerusalem. You have one week to comply. Once that has been accomplished to the Angel's satisfaction, all residents of New Jerusalem, including the new residents from *Hope,* will surrender all weapons to the army of the Angel. You have two days to comply after the relocation of the people from *Hope.* Lastly, all documents in your possession relating to Oak Ridge National Lab will be made available to the Angel within the next twenty-four hours. Failure to comply with any of the three demands by the specified deadline will result in instant annihilation. Do you understand the Angel's demands as I have stated them?" He smiled broadly as he waited.

Without hesitation or consulting with the Moses, SSP Simon pulled an ancient revolver from under his shirt and shot the major six times in the chest and the head.

Everyone else in the room sat stunned, first by the major's demands, but more by the SSP's response. Everyone was stunned except me. For my part, it was the only logical response. We were going to war.

The Moses

I couldn't believe what just happened. I finally stood and shouted at the SSP. "What have you done, Simon? In God's name, what have you done?!"

I was surprised to see both the SSP and the lieutenant commander turn their backs toward the vid com to face me and put their index fingers to their lips. I was puzzled by their reaction, but waited until Simon whispered in my ear, "We are being monitored by the enemy. Please play along. Yell at me again."

I continued yelling, "Don't come begging for forgiveness from me. You are such a fool. You've signed our death warrants. Get out of my sight, both of you."

I turned abruptly and headed for my private office, the two of them following and beseaching me to forgive them. I hoped we weren't over acting our parts. I entered my office with them on my heels, and slammed the door behind them. I touched a button on my desk and prayed our jamming system was adequate to mask our conversation.

Simon spoke first. "It was a bluff, Your Highness, a way of getting what they wanted without having to actually fight. I believe their main objective is access to the ancient's lab. Taking possession of *Hope* is a secondary objective. I think taking New Jerusalem is only a means to an end—getting to the lab."

I looked at Hiroshi, and saw him nodding his head vigorously. "I completely agree with Simon." He quickly turned his head toward the SSP and asked, "Is it okay for me to call you Simon?"

Simon grinned at him and said, "Absolutely, if I may call you Hiroshi."

I thought how strange the world was becoming, how quickly deadly enemies were becoming friendly.

Hiroshi said, "I must contact *Hope* and make both our leaders aware of what happened immediately. I can't use the vid com, I'm positive our enemy is monitoring all our communications. I need to beam back as soon as I can. Why don't you kick me out of your office and tell me to never return, or something like that. I would highly recommend you order Simon to try and contact the Angel and grovel, ask for forgiveness for killing his major."

I nodded once and stood up. I walked to the door and threw it open so hard it slammed against the wall and bounced back, but Hiroshi was backing out making bowing motions as he went. I screamed at him as he went. "This is your fault, all your fault! If you hadn't come up with that damned kidnapping scheme, none of this would have happened. Get out of my sight and never come back!" He turned and ran for the balcony. In an instant the beam picked him up and returned him to his ship.

I turned back to Simon and bellowed at him, "I can't believe you shot that man. Look at the danger you've put us in. Get on the vid com and try to contact the Angel and beg his forgiveness. Tell him we will comply with all his wishes. And consider yourself demoted. You are no longer the SSP, not even an SP. You are back to being a protector. I don't want to see you again for a long, long time!" I slammed my door, moved around my desk and fell back into my chair. I began to smile, then chuckled. *When I retire from being the Moses, perhaps I will take up acting.*

Captain David Lawrence

I was sound asleep when my com chimed. "Answer," I managed to mumble. "This better be damned important."

"It is, sir. This is Hiroshi. Sorry to wake you but this is an emergency. We've made contact with the army's commander. We are almost certain he has tapped our com channels. I need to brief you, the XO, and the governor as soon as possible in a secured room."

I was wide awake at the word emergency. "I'll contact the governor and the XO, we'll meet you in Room A in twenty minutes. Order coffee and donuts." I broke contact, contacted the governor and the XO, and scrambled to get ready. Miriam almost woke up and asked me why I was making so much noise in the middle of the night. I told her it was an emergency. She mumbled something unintelligible and went back to sleep.

We all walked into Room A with a minute to spare. We left our personal coms in a lockbox outside the door while the security team did a quick sweep of the room for any surveillance devices. The room was clean and we entered, Hiroshi secured the door as the governor and I poured coffee, took a pastry and sat down. Hiroshi joined us and the briefing began.

"We kidnapped four of the enemy as you approved. Three were grunts and one was a major. The grunts didn't know much and had varied backgrounds. They didn't even know the names of their leaders. According to a corporal they rotated leaders frequently, but he identified them as second lieutenants. I'm pretty sure the grunts are all locals, initially scavengers, but now well trained foot soldiers. We also think the army headcount is around five thousand troops, not the ten thousand we originally estimated."

"That's a big difference, why the change?" I asked.

"Our original estimate was assuming the troop transports were full, but when we surveyed the campsite at night and did a headcount, it gave us the lower number," Hiroshi answered.

"The major was a different story. He knew all about us, New Jerusalem and *Hope*. He knew my name and rank and even said hello in Japanese. He knew the SP had just been promoted to Senior Security Priest."

"How could he know that?" I asked.

Hiroshi held up a hand. "It will all become clear in a moment. He told us the commander of the army was a man who called himself The Angel of Death and he was also the leader of the Generation Ship *Faith,* except now it's called *The Avenging Angel.*" After Hirosh spelled out the demands he ended with the Angel's threat: If we fail to comply with any of the demands we will all be annihilated immediately. The Governor and XO looked as shocked as I felt.

The governor asked, "What happened next?"

"The SSP shot and killed the major right on the spot. Shot him six times with an old revolver."

"Why did he do that?" asked the XO.

"We think it was all a setup. The major was a plant. He was the last one to be grabbed. They were expecting us. The Moses, the SSP and I agree this was a bluff. What they really want is what we want, access to the ancient's lab. We think they were intercepting all our communications between New Jerusalem and *Hope* and knew about our kidnapping plan. That's why I wanted this meeting in a secured room. I recommend the first thing we do is search for *Faith.* I know she was reported lost, but maybe she wasn't. Send out recon drones or shuttles. If she didn't crash, she's probably in the same condition we're in, a little worse since she is older. I really don't know much about *Faith's* mission. The second would be to see if we can figure out who the Angle of Death really is. I think it's a remote possibility, but maybe we can negotiate with him and avoid a war. One last thing. I would recommend we be prepared for a possible attack on *Hope.* If *Faith* is really still in orbit, I wouldn't put it past this leader to attack on two fronts, both *Hope* and New Jerusalem, possibly simultaneously." Hiroshi sat back and waited for our reaction.

The governor spoke first. "Captain, based on what I just heard, I believe this falls under your jurisdiction, I will be more than happy to assist you wherever you think I might be able to help."

"I agree, governor." I turned to Hiroshi and said, "Thank you for the quick response and your recommendations. I will implement your suggestions immediately."

I turned to Hiroshi as we left the room and gathered our personal coms. "You need to get some rest. I'll take it from here. Get with me and the XO at 0900 hours tomorrow morning." He started to protest, I cut him off. "I want you rested and alert. It's going to be a busy day tomorrow. You're dismissed. And hey! Good job this evening."

SSP Simon

Before I attempted to contact the Angel … I really hate that name, from now on I will refer to him as the enemy leader … I decided to have Dr. Sanborn present. The Moses told me Dr. Sanborn set up the vid com system that *Hope* beamed to us. If I was able to contact the … the enemy leader, I wanted someone with computer tech knowledge observing.

He arrived very quickly after I commed him. He looked pensive, but then I realized he probably thought I was going to punish him for assembling the com system. I assured him there would be no punishment, unless he refused to assist me now. He readily agreed to help. He showed me how to initiate a com link on a broadband signal. Anyone with a similar vid com system would hear and see my message.

In my most groveling voice I began. "This is former Senior Security Priest Simon attempting to contact the … the Angel of Death aboard the generation ship *The Avenging Angel.* Please reply." I waited for a full minute, but the screen remained blank. I looked at Dr. Sanborn, but he just shook his head indicating no contact.

I tried three more times with similar results. I was just about to give up, when the screen flared to life.

The image was of a man, a huge man who appeared extremely angry. He was wearing an admiral's uniform that was way too small for him. His face was contorted in rage and he screamed at me, "Protector Simon!!! You are a dead man! Any chance you had for survival vanished when you assassinated my ambassador. You killed him with six shots from your puny ancient pistol. He died instantly from the first shot. The other five were a waste of ammunition. Your death will not be so pleasant and it won't be quick, I assure you of that." His voice had changed from a roar to almost a whisper, a deep whisper that sent chills up my spine. I lowered my head so I could no longer see his face. He had one blue eye and one brown, it made my stomach churn.

With my head bowed, I said, "I know my life is forfeit, but please don't punish New Jerusalem for my crime. In God's name, I beg you, spare them." I ended with a sob.

I was surprised at his answer. "In God's name? You ask me in God's name? There is no God!" he screamed. "You will all die in a nuclear holocaust that will make the ten plagues Moses visited upon the Egyptians look like a sunny day in spring."

I was surprised when the Moses spoke up from behind me. I had no idea he was there. "Actually, they were God's plagues, Moses only told Pharaoh they were coming if he did not let the slaves go free."

His eyes searched his screen, stopping when they were locked on the Moses with those mismatched colored eyes. "You dare to correct me?" he roared. "Who do you think you are to correct me?"

"I'm a servant of the God you claim does not exist. Tell me, how can you call yourself an angel if there is no God? God created the angels just as he created humans. If there is no God, there can be no angels. Therefore you don't exist. You are a fake. Leave us. Bother us no more."

The screen went dark.

Now I was the one to stand open mouthed in disbelief. "Your Holiness! What have you done?"

I looked at Dr. Sanborn, who stood behind the Moses, trying to suppress his laughter. The Moses was beginning to smile now. "Will someone tell me what is going on?" I said. I was getting irritated. I was the only one in the room who didn't get the joke.

Dr. Sanborn spoke first, "May I speak, Your Grace?" The Moses nodded and Dr. Sanborn composed himself and said, "It wasn't real. The moment he appeared on the screen, I could tell it was an avatar, and not a very good one. Even the voice was processed to have a scary effect."

The Moses took over. "His threat to destroy New Jerusalem with a nuclear bomb made no sense either. I think we all agree his main objective is access to the ancient's lab. If he destroys New Jerusalem with a nuclear bomb, he destroys the lab as well. He may be stupid, but not that stupid."

I thought about interrupting the Moses and mention he didn't say *when* he would destroy New Jerusalem, maybe it was after he had taken what he needed from the lab.

The Moses paused for a moment then added, "Besides, I know who he is. While you were engaged in conversation with the supposed Angel of Death, I received a message on an encrypted com from the *Hope*. They were watching the discussion on their vid com system as well. It seems when they saw our enemy, he had one blue eye and one brown, the *Hope's* chaplain recognized him. He is the chaplain from the generation ship *Faith*."

Chaplain Byron George

We were all gathered in *Hope's* main conference room as I rose and walked to the rostrum at the head of the table. It was my first chance to meet the Moses from New Jerusalem and a few of his associates. Senior Security Priest Simon sat next to him on his right side and the head of their IT department, Dr. John Sanborn sat to his left. Behind the Moses were two additional protectors.

Hope was represented by the usual group: Captain Lawrence, Commander White, the XO, Governor Stewart, Quartermaster Taylor, Lieutenant Commander Koyama, his wife Anna, and an assortment of crew from the Beam Room, Flight Control, and Command Center. My immediate job had little to do with my role as chaplain. I was to inform them of everything I knew about the chaplain of the generation ship *Faith*. "Ladies and Gentlemen, I'm Chaplain Byron George, today I'll share with you everything I know regarding the man who now calls himself The Angel of Death.

"About a year ago, I received a com system hail from Commander Frederick Dekker, the chaplain of the generation ship *Faith*. Prior to this hail, I had never spoken to the chaplain or even been aware of his existence. At the time of his hail, *Faith* was approximately one year out from Earth, one year ahead of *Hope* traveling along the same course. At that distance, together with our speed, the delay time between messages was a little over eighteen days."

The Moses raised his hand and asked, "Did you say days?"

"Yes, Your Holiness, days. From the time I received his message until he could get my reply would be a total of thirty-six days, over a month. That makes it very difficult to carry on a conversation. You record a message, send it off and wait to get a reply. A lot can happen in a month. Usually, messages sent over that distance, at that speed are quite lengthy and the ship's com system automatically records them so they can be replayed as needed. His message was about a half hour in duration. I'm not going to replay his entire message during this meeting, however we will make it available to you all so you can watch it whenever it is convenient. I'll show you the first few minutes which I believe is sufficient for you to get the flavor of the message."

Everyone focused their attention on the vid screen. The date and time stamp showed up in the upper right corner. A man sat very close to the screen and began speaking in a whisper. "I hope and pray this message is delivered to chaplain Byron George aboard the generation ship *Hope*. My name is Frederick Dekker, the chaplain of *Faith*. I know we don't know each other, but I don't know who else to try. I've tried to hail Earth so many times I've lost count. I hope someone, somewhere, receives this and passes it on to whomever is in charge, assuming there's somebody left. My fear is The Plague decimated the Earth and there is no civilization left."

He paused and looked over his shoulder. There were unintelligible voices shouting in the background, but after a few seconds they stopped and chaplain Dekker continued. "Everything is in disarray here. We're one step away from complete chaos."

There was a tremendous crashing sound followed by people screaming in pain. The recording stopped. A few seconds later it began again. The time stamp indicated thirty-three minutes had elapsed, but chaplain Dekker continued as if there had never been any interruption, let alone any explanation as to what had happened.

"Things are getting worse. We spent almost two years exploring the other two stars in the Alpha Centauri cluster. It was believed there could be habitable planets orbiting both stars, however, our examination did not turn up any planet that would support human life. We did actually find life on a few planets, but nothing more complex then various forms of bacteria. Sample were taken and stored in cold storage to be studied after our return. We had brief contact with *Hope* during the last half of our mission, mostly to update crew changes and exchange information on research activities. You must have records of these updates in your computer system. Halfway through the fifth generation, things started to go bad. Equipment began to breakdown or malfunction even though their scheduled maintenance was strictly maintained.

Then crops started to fail. Animals started coming down with strange diseases. By the end of the fifth generation, chickens became extinct. We had no source for eggs to restart our livestock population. We had to go on half rations five years ago. Food was spoiling at an alarming rate. It was as if God had abandoned us. Slowly at first, very gradually, people stopped coming to worship service. I started calling on long time dedicated believers, but many of them would not even acknowledge my presence. The attitude became, if God doesn't answer our prayers, what good is he? There came a time when no one showed up at the chapel. No one came to ask me to pray for them. I thought I had reached the very end of my rope. I was wrong. The riots began, chaos became complete. The ship's captain declared martial law, however before it went into effect, the acting governor had him assassinated! That occurred two weeks ago. Last week I heard reports many were resorting to cannibalism. I don't think I can hold out much longer. I feel like Christ on the Cross. 'My God, my God, Why hast thou forsaken me?'"

I froze the picture of chaplain Dekker's face. His blue and brown eyes were clearly visible.

The conference room was dead quiet. After a few moments, the Moses asked the question many were asking themselves. "How could he have possibly survived that ordeal? How could all of those things go wrong at the same time? This is beyond tragic. No wonder the poor soul went insane. It's a miracle he even survived."

SSP Simon asked softly, "Did you have any further contact with him?"

"I replied to his message. I tried to encourage him to look forward to an eternal life in the hereafter, to be honest, if I were on the receiving end of that message, it would have been meaningless to me. He never acknowledged my reply and I never heard from him again. I assumed he died with the rest of the souls on *Faith.* Apparently, he didn't. I informed Captain Lawrence of the message. I'm sure he is better qualified to give you information on any follow-up."

The Moses looked around the table then said to all of us, "On behalf of those gathered here, I'd like to thank you for your presentation, Chaplain George. I can't imagine how difficult that must have been for you the first time you heard it. It probably was just as disheartening to go through it again. Before we continue, I would like us to offer a silent prayer for all those tormented souls, and ask God to forgive their transgressions and receive them into His arms."

Everyone bowed their heads, and for a few minutes, silent prayers were made. When the Moses said, "Thank you all," there wasn't a dry eye in the room.

Captain David Lawrence

I waited for the Moses to finish, then walked to the rostrum to continue our briefing. "We were able to track *Faith* all the way back to Earth. All attempts to contact them were unsuccessful. The data suggests the ship decelerated to orbit insertion velocity and had actually begun to orbit. We tracked it up until the time it disappeared behind the Earth. We were never able to reacquire it once it disappeared. The assumption was that somewhere on the backside it lost orbit integrity and crashed. *Faith* was one of the two largest space ships ever built, *Hope* was the other. It was so large, it wouldn't burn up on re-entry. Analysis predicted it crashed somewhere in the Gobi Desert in what used to be called China. However, we were unable to find any crash debris. It should have left a considerable crash signature, but we were unable to detect it."

The SSP raised his hand and I acknowledged him. "Captain, If *Faith* crashed into the Gobi Desert, how did Chaplain Dekker survive?"

"Our best guess, and it's an educated guess, is some of the crew must have left *Faith* in shuttles before it entered Earth's atmosphere. Assuming their compliment of shuttles was the same as ours, their largest shuttle could have accommodated fifty passengers. At best, they had three shuttles with this capacity. They probably had several smaller shuttles as we do. The question would be, how many qualified pilots did they have that could maneuver the shuttles from space to land safely on Earth. That takes considerable talent. I'm sure the chaplain was not able to fly a shuttle let alone make a re-entry and safe landing. With all the chaos on the ship, I would be surprised if there was more than one shuttle that made it safely. Ever since the chaplain's reappearance, we've been actively searching to determine where the shuttles may have landed. Unfortunately the Earth is a big target. We're focusing our search mainly on the northeastern part of what used to be the United States. We are also looking at possible locations for the Angel's training base. We are looking for old army camp locations that could have been used as a training base. We believe the army was formed at a single site. They used that site to accumulate a large enough number of soldiers to carry out the attack. They were probably trained there, planned their attack and was the point of departure for their trip southward. It's difficult to believe that a former chaplain with no command experience could be the leader of an army. He must have had the help of several other *Faith* crew members. We also believe a smaller verion of this army existed before *Faith* returned to Earth. Whoever led that older army had the help of combat trained refugees from *Faith*. There is much we don't know. What we do know is that a sizable army is moving on New Jerusalem. It is led by someone who calls himself the Angel of Death. We need to stop him and his army! It's been suggested he may be in the armored command vehicle. However it appears he was in some type of building or studio when he vid commed the SSP. Let me be clear. There are a lot of things we don't know. I promise you we're going to find answers and soon. It is tragic what happened to *Faith* and the pain and suffering their people went through, but we will not let them continue to hurt us. New Jerusalem will not fall."

SSP Simon

When we returned to New Jerusalem, I requested Dr. Sanborn come to my new office. I have to thank the Moses for his generosity in providing me with these new accommodations along with my promotion. The new office is much more spacious and offers complete privacy when I so desire. At this moment that was exactly what I desired. Dr. Sanborn knocked twice on the opened door. I motioned for him to enter and take a seat at my small, but adequate, conference table. "Dr. Sanborn, I need your computer expertise on a matter of some importance, at least important to me."

"Certainly, SSP. How can I help?"

"I want to determine if the account we heard and saw on the vid com from *Faith's* chaplain was ... how can I put this delicately? I want to see if he was lying to us."

Sanborn looked skeptical. "You think he was lying? He seemed so sincere."

"Yes. Yes he did, and maybe he was. However, since I'm an investigator I have certain responsibilities. I think it is my duty to never take anything at face value unless there is no other option. In this case I believe there is an option. I'm just not sure how to go about it. That's where you come in. I was given a copy of the chaplain's full report. We have a computer application that allows us the ability to determine if someone is lying. However, I've only used it in live situations, not on a recording over a year old. Would it be possible to play the recording and have the computer determine if the person speaking is telling the truth?"

Dr. Sanborn didn't hesitate. "Yes, SSP. How soon do you need the analysis? Oh, and one other question. Do you want just a general answer, such as 'the subject told six lies during this recording.' Or do you want a answer on each and every sentence?"

"By all means, I want the latter. I can never have enough details. While I'm at it, I need this to be done in isolation. If it turns out he lied in the majority of the things he said, I'll make it known to everyone as well as your part in providing the information. On the other hand, if he was telling the truth, I don't want people to think I was out on a witch hunt."

Dr. Sanborn nodded and said, "I'll have your results by the end of the day."

Captain David Lawrence

It's a good thing we decided to hold daily meetings. Things were happening so quickly, it was imperative everybody was kept informed. Today's meeting was being held in the Moses' conference room, a part of the Temple offices. A contingency from *Hope* beamed down a few minutes before the meeting started and we watched as a Temple security detail swept the room for any possible listening devices. The room was clean. Ever since we discovered the communication between the Temple and *Hope* had been compromised, it became a standard practice to be sure similar future compromises didn't occur.

Our group included Lieutenant Commander Koyama and representatives from the Beam Room and Flight Control. New Jerusalem was represented by the Moses, SSP Simon and Dr. Sanborn. SSP Simon led the meeting.

"Good morning, everyone. We have a full agenda, let's get started. I'll lead off. Dr. Sanborn and I have made a very interesting discovery regarding the vid com we watched yesterday from Chaplain Dekker, currently known as The Angel of Death. It turns out, almost everything he said in his vid message to *Hope's* Chaplain George was a lie."

That brought some looks of surprise on most of the faces in the room, including myself. Apparently, the Moses was also just finding out this news. He looked as surprised as the rest of us. He asked SSP Simon, "Could you please share with us how you made this startling discovery?"

The SSP replied, "Of course, Your Grace. Some of you may not be aware that we have a computer program that can tell when a suspect is lying to us. It has come in very handy when we are interrogating someone suspected of a sin. Hiroshi, I believe you have firsthand experience with this software?"

Hiroshi grimaced as he remembered the questioning he had been subjected to. "That's correct Simon. You used it on me several times to see if I was lying to you about losing my memory. It was quite accurate."

The SSP paused considering Hiroshi comments. His tone softened as he said, "My experience was limited to using the software when interrogating a live subject in real time. I asked Dr. Sanborn to see if he could modify the software so it could be used with a recording of a suspect, the suspect in this case being Chaplain Dekker. Dr. Sanborn could you please share with us the results of your efforts?"

Dr. Sanborn said, "It was really a trivial matter to adjust the software to accurately determine when a person in a recording is lying. Once the updates were completed, we ran twenty test cases and the results were successful 100% of the time. I then applied the modified software to analyze Chaplain Dekker's message. Almost everything he said was untrue. We analyzed every single sentence of the full message for its truthfulness and the results were, he was lying 94.5% of the time. There was one notable exception. The last three sentences that were presented in the vid were: 'I don't think I can hold on much longer. I feel like Christ on the cross. 'My God, my God, why hast thou forsaken me?' Those were not lies. He truly believed what he said. We have data cubes for each of you that provide a sentence by sentence analysis. Of course, for security reasons, the data is encrypted."

Everyone sat quietly trying to determine the reasons for the chaplain to lie. What did he hope to gain. Was he deranged? Was it some type of plot? I said, "Well, that was certainly a bombshell." It was going to take some serious thought to realize the full ramifications of the chaplain's lies. For one thing, no one would ever trust what he said. For another, any compassion we may have felt toward him died.

During the rest of the meeting a couple of other interesting facts were presented. The first one was Flight Operations discovered the location of a shuttle that ferried survivors of *Faith* to a safe landing. It was found in a barren field in what used to be called Upper State New York. A team from *Hope* was beamed down to investigate. Attempts had been made to hide the shuttle, but over time, the shielding deteriorated. Inspection of the shuttle revealed the decomposed bodies of three people strapped into passenger seats. Cause of death was not determined.

The second item of interest had to do with *Hope's* beaming capacity. It was suggested we might attempt to beam the tanks from the battlefield and somehow disable them. Unfortunately, the Abrams M1A4-Mod 7 weighs about 70 tons or 140,000 pounds, almost three times the beam's lifting limit of 50,000 pounds. However, the good news was that the M1139 Armored Command Vehicle weighs a little over 18 tons or 36,000 pounds, well within the limits of the beam. We would have to consider what we want to do with the command vehicle, especially since some believed the Angel of Death was inside.

A suggestion was made that we beam the command vehicle into the Temple courtyard and force whoever was inside to come out. There was a resounding No! to that idea from the Moses. He questioned, "What if the command vehicle is a Trojan Horse full of explosives. It could destroy the Temple and kill hundreds of the Chosen!"

Needless to say, the location in that plan was dropped, but other locations were still on the table. Suggestions were made for a big open field, miles from the army. We could surround it with our troops and force them to surrender. Another option to consider was to beam it into space. The command vehicle is not air tight and does not carry a separate air supply. We could leave it in space long enough for anyone inside to suffocate, then return it to Earth and identify the bodies inside.

They were all considered possible approaches, however everyone agreed it needed further study. Unfortunately, the army was only three days from New Jerusalem. We needed to decide soon, very soon.

We adjourned the meeting and my team beamed back to *Hope*.

XO Henry White

I was on the bridge and had command of the ship while the captain was down in New Jerusalem for a meeting. I was drinking my cup of coffee, thinking about what I was going to do during my next workout in the gym when the communications officer spoke up. "XO I've got a distress call from a shuttle."

I set my coffee down and replied, "I wasn't aware we had launched a shuttle today."

"We didn't, XO. It's not one of ours. It's one of *Faith's* shuttles."

That got my complete attention, no more daydreaming about a 500 pound bench press. "Put it on speaker," I ordered.

"This is Light Shuttle 2 from gen ship *Faith*, calling *Hope*. We are declaring an emergency, over!"

"Roger Light Shuttle 2, this is Commander White, XO of the *Hope*. Please state the nature of your emergency, over."

"We are seeking asylum, over."

"Please identify the people requesting asylum, over."

"Only two of us. I'm the pilot, Lieutenant Cross. I have one passenger, Chaplain Dekker."

That set off warning bells in my head. "Are you currently being pursued?"

"No sir, but it is just a matter of time."

I could hear the fear in his voice. "Is your shuttle armed?"

"No sir."

"Do either of you have personal weapons?"

There was a short pause. "No sir."

"Excuse me for not trusting you. We will be running a weapons scan before granting asylum." I nodded to the communication officer to begin the scan. A minute later he indicated the shuttle was clean.

"Light Shuttle 2, you are cleared to enter the aft shuttle bay on the port side of the ship. You are to remain in your ship with your hatch sealed. A security team will board you shortly for inspection. *Hope* out."

So much for my morning workout. "Com, has the captain returned from his meeting?"

"Yes sir. He just beamed up."

"Please request his presence on the bridge ASAP."

"Aye, XO. Requesting the Captain's presence on the bridge."

Captain David Lawrence

I was almost to my quarters when the bridge commed me. The XO wanted to meet with me as quickly as possible. If it was that important, I decided to com Hiroshi and have him join us. Hiroshi beat me there and had a message from his wife. Anna and Miriam want us to meet them in the gym when our meeting was over. I shook my head, *don't they realize we are almost at war?* Then I sighed, *it won't take more than an hour and we need a short distraction. Besides, who's going to spot the XO on his 500 pound bench press?"* The three of us went into my ready room, located just behind the bridge. The XO explained the asylum request from Chaplain Dekker and his pilot. All I could think was, *our lives are full of so many surprises, most of them not good.* After a brief discussion, I said, "Here's what I want to do. Have them sit in their shuttle for thirty minutes before the security guards unseal the hatch and inspects them. Have an explosives team make a very thorough search of the shuttle's exterior for any kind of booby trap. Let them think we're debating whether to grant them asylum or not. Then have the security team take them to Secure Room A and sit for another thirty minutes with armed guards inside the room. Make sure we record any conversation between the chaplain and the pilot. We need to contact the SSP and the Moses to see if they want to join us. Also, invite Chaplain George as well."

The XO asked, "What are we going to be doing for the next hour?"

"Did you bring your gym bag?" I asked

A smile began to form on his face. "Always have it with me, cap."

"We'll meet you in the gym in five minutes. I can't wait to see this record setting bench press. Besides," I gestured to Hiroshi, "our wives are expecting us."

Miriam

Anna and I arrived at the gym before the men. The gym was nearly empty due to the ship being on alert status. This was Anna's fourth trip to the gym and it had always been just the two of us when we went. I was surprised at how strong she was and how quickly she took to the exercises I showed her. If I had the time, I would do some type of workout every day. I really prefered yoga and tried to attend classes three times a week. On the off days, I did some light weight training. I suggested that routine to Anna, and it fit her like a glove. Today, since the men would be joining us, we did some warm up stretches and prepared to do some weight training. Henry was the first to come out of the men's locker room. He had on a tank top that displayed his ample muscles. I asked him if he wore that shirt to show everyone how big and muscular he was. He said no, he didn't want a shirt to restrict his movements. No matter what he said, I knew he wanted everyone to see he was the biggest dude in the gym. Those were his words, not mine. I'm not sure what a dude is. Henry likes to speak in what he calls Old English. Hiroshi and David (I like to call him my captain) came in together and started doing some warm ups while Henry set up the bar. I noticed when he was doing what he called "moving some serious iron;" he was all business. He really focused on completing every lift. Hiroshi and my captain put two big plates on the bar (135 pounds) as warm up weight. Anna and I watched as they both did ten repetitions. Anna looked very impressed. Then Henry doubled the plates on the bar and did ten reps of his own. I noticed he wasn't even sweating or breathing hard. Hiroshi added 50 pounds and he and David did eight reps. Henry added two more big plates and did six more reps.

Anna and I decided we were just going to become spectators today. She leaned over and whispered to me, "Did you notice his chest and arms are getting bigger each time he lifts? His arms are bigger than my legs."

I whispered back, "It's called getting pumped."

Our men added more weight, Hiroshi did six reps. David did five but couldn't finish his sixth rep. Henry had been standing behind him and when he saw the bar wasn't going up anymore, he reached over and grabbed it with one hand and put it back on the rack. David said, "That's enough for me."

Henry added two more plates and did an easy set of four. "He's getting more pumped," Anna said. "I hope he doesn't explode." She sounded genuinely worried.

Hiroshi said he was done too. Henry walked over to the water cooler and took a drink. He reached into his gym bag and pulled out a block of chalk and began coating his hands. He said to David and Hiroshi, "Load the bar to 540, please. Gonna try a single. Need you both to spot."

They loaded the bar and Dave got to one end of the bar and Hiroshi to the other. Henry positioned himself on the bench and began taking very deep, noisy breaths. After the third breath he gave a loud shout and lifted the bar from the rack to an overhead position with his arms locked out. He brought the bar down slowly until it touched his chest then, with a mighty roar thrust the bar straight up and locked it out again. "Take it!" he yelled and

Dave and Hiroshi grabbed the ends of the bar and helped guide it back to the rack. I could see Henry's chest rising and falling as he took in more air. He had a big smile on his face. "That was my personal best and set a record for *Hope*. Best bench in two hundred years. I can die happy."

SSP Simon

Before the meeting began I pulled the captian aside for a privated conversation. "No matter what is said in this meeting, we have to consider this is a trap of somekind. You may think I'm being paranoid, but we need to be extremely careful. This man has lied to us before, so pardon me if I'm suspect of what he says. In addition, I respectfully request you have backup plans in case they are planning some type of sabotage."

The captain seemed to be processing what I said. When he answered he said, "You're right, SSP. We need to be prepared for the worst."

Chaplain Byron George

There were nine of us gathered around the conference table; the Moses, SSP Simon, and Dr. Sanborn from New Jerusalem, the pilot and Chaplain Dekker from *Faith,* and the captain, XO, Lieutenant Commander Koyama and myself from *Hope*. Captain Lawrence made the introductions and I was asked to begin the discussion.

"Chaplain Dekker, I want you to know we reviewed your message to me while *Faith* was about one year from Earth. New Jerusalem has a computer program that can determine if someone is not telling the truth. Dr. Sanborn used that computer program to analyze your message and determined most of what you said was not true. That computer program is now active and will signal if any statements made in this room are not true. Let me demonstrate. XO, would you tell us a lie, please?"

The XO thought for a moment, then said, "I hate weight training."

Immediately a soft woman's voice said, "That statement is not true."

I turned back to Chaplain Dekker and said, "Do you understand how it works?" The chaplain nodded his head. I resumed speaking, "I have been asked to tell you, if you intentionally lie during this meeting, your request for asylum will be denied and you will be placed in the brig for the remainder of this conflict. Do you understand?"

He nodded his head. I said, "Please answerer yes or no."

"Yes, I understand. I will tell you the truth."

"Then let us begin. I have a series of questions that I will ask you. When I'm done, others at the table will also ask you questions. Lieutenant Cross, you're the pilot of the shuttle?"

"Yes sir, I am."

"You may also be asked questions and the same rules apply. Do you understand?"

"Yes sir, I do."

"First question, Chaplain Dekker, why are you seeking asylum?"

"I was afraid for my life if I stayed with the army."

I waited briefly, but the computer did not interrupt. "Second question, who do you think would have you killed?"

"The leader of the army. He calls himself the Angel of Death."

"Aren't you the Angel of Death? Aren't you the one in the vid, threatening our annihilation if we don't surrender?"

"No, I swear that was not me! That was the Angel. Actually, it was an avatar created by a tech. He gave the avatar one blue and one brown eye to make you think it was me."

There was no signal of a lie.

"Is the Angel one of the crew from *Faith?*"

"No, listen, I believe this would go a lot faster if you let me tell you what happened. You can ask me all your questions if I leave anything out. Please let me do that."

I looked at Captain Lawrence who nodded, then at the Moses and he also nodded and said, "Yes, let him tell his story. This is all being recorded, isn't it?"

"Absolutely," said Captain Lawrence.

I turned to Chaplain Dekker and said, "All right chaplain tell us your story, please begin with the message you sent me from *Faith.*"

Chaplain Frederick Dekker

"*Faith* left Earth about a year before *Hope.* Of course I wasn't alive at the time, but all this information was in the ship's log. I will let you know when I'm recounting personal experiences. We were already clear of the Solar System on our way to the Alpha Centauri cluster when we received news of The Plague. As we received more and more information, unrest increased. A large percentage of *Faith's* original population wanted to go back. But the captain and the governor both agreed there was nothing they could do and we pressed on. We were on our third generation when we arrived at Alpha Centauri. We didn't find any planet where human life could survive. We didn't have the resources to terraform any of the planets we discovered. The unrest among our population was continuing to grow. It took four years for a communication signal from Earth to reach Alpha Centauri. We'd been gone a hundred years and hadn't heard anything from Earth since the last of the second generation had passed away. A movement arose within the third generation called Repopulate the Earth. The RE supporters said *Faith's* mission was to ensure the human race survived. They believed the best way to do that was to return to Earth as fast as we could and stop the chaos, to regenerate civilization on a world that wouldn't require any terraforming at all. All we needed to do was to establish a pocket of civilization and nurture it into a worldwide civilization. They believed that The Plague had to have run its course and Earth was just waiting for us to save it. The third generation crew found a way to increase our speed to almost ten percent the speed of light. They projected it would decrease our flight time to Earth in half. The engineers said the risk of traveling at that speed was manageable. Instead of staying at Alpha Centauri for a year or two, we were there for only six months. Then we headed home to save our home planet.

"Everything went well at first. The third generation passed away and was replaced by the fourth who welcomed our new mission with open arms. They estimated we would reach Earth while the oldest fourth generationist was middle-aged. Our mantra became Save the Earth.

"I became the chaplain and was caught up in the fervor. Attendance at the chapel was at an all time high. It was God's will for us to return to His creation, the place where mankind was intended to live, not on some dark inhospitable rock, generations removed from home. We were almost there, so close we could see it on long range vid, only another year to go. That's when things went bad.

"The third generation engineers had been overly optimistic. Our EM propulsion system began to fail. The nuclear reactors had reached their end. The reaction mass was almost gone with no hope to acquire more.

"It was discovered traveling at the higher speed had resulted in microscopic particles impinging on the ship's surface, eroding the shielding that protected us from dangerous interstellar radiation. The increased radiation levels resulted in more and more crop failures. Food animals began dying from cancers. That's when the rioting began. Martial law was declared, and for a time, things appeared to be trending back toward normalcy. That trend lasted for only a few weeks as the ship's systems continued to degrade.

"The best estimates were that we might be able to coast to Earth in a little less than a year, but the food supply wouldn't last that long. More importantly, our air freshers were beginning to fail; the carbon dioxide was building at an alarming rate.

"I sat in on a meeting of the ship's officers and saw the evilness of man begin to emerge. The captain said there was no way we could save everyone, therefore he would decided who would live and who would die. Our mission to save civilization was still intact, but we would have to do it with fewer people. He went on to say there was no possibility of placing the ship in orbit, but when we were close to reaching orbital altitude we would launch all our shuttles which would allow us to save approximately five hundred people. The rest of the five thousand would perish during re-entry. To soften the remark, he said that many of those not chosen would have died by then anyway, so it wasn't as bad as it sounded.

"I felt nauseous. I wanted to stand up and scream at the inhumanity of what he said, but deep down I was hoping I would be one of the chosen. So I sat quietly. We were supposed to keep this all secret to prevent an uprising, but the word got out and the riots began again.

"Sometime after that, I commed you with my message. I was out of my mind with fear and self-loathing. I said whatever popped into my head. I couldn't believe God was going to let this happen, that He wouldn't intercede in some fashion. After all, weren't we attempting to do His bidding by returning to Earth to save civilization? It was at that moment I decided there really must not be a God after all. For surely, if there was, he would see the righteousness of our actions and save us, not just a token five hundred, but all of us. As we approached orbital altitude, the chosen had sequestered themselves inside the shuttles and blocked the entrances into the shuttle bays. On a given signal, the outside doors opened and one by one the shuttles deserted *Faith* and made their way to the Earth's surface. Not all made it safely. No one had flown the shuttles for years and the inexperience of the pilots cost many their lives. I believe only two of the large shuttles made it safely to Earth. It was hard to tell, we landed in the middle of a rainstorm. I never saw any of the other shuttles or their passengers. I assumed, other than the hundred from our two shuttles, the others died."

Chaplain Byron George

When Frederick paused to take a drink of water I made a decision and said, "I think it would be a good point to take a break. Are there any objections?" There were none and many got up to use the restroom or to get something to drink. Both the chaplin and the pilot left for the restroom as well. No one approached Chaplain Dekker. They were all waiting to hear the rest of his story. After the break and everyone had returned to their seats, I asked, "Are there any questions regarding the material that was presented so far?"

"Yes, I have a question for Lieutenant Cross," said Hiroshi. "Chaplain Dekker mentioned he was only aware of two large shuttles making it to Earth. Yet you showed up in a small shuttle. Were you the pilot that flew that shuttle from orbit to Earth?"

The lieutenant sat up straighter and replied, "Yes sir, I was the pilot that made the re-entry flight. The small shuttle holds six people including the pilot. Usually we would fly it with a copilot, but none were chosen to make the re-entry flights."

"Who were your passengers on your re-entry flight?" asked the SSP.

"I really don't know, sir. I was the last one to board and I was busy with the preflight check. Once we launched, I was very busy with flying the bird, especially during the storm when we got down into the atmosphere."

Captain Lawrence asked, "Were you the pilot flying the F-35B who shot down our shuttle?"

"No sir, I was not. To the best of my knowledge, the F-35B pilots were part of the army, not from *Faith.*" There were no more questions and I turned it back over to Chaplain Dekker.

Chaplain Frederick Dekker

"The landing was rough and it was raining very hard. I was very shaken by the flight and wanted to remain in the shuttle. Several of us chose to stay, hoping the rain would subside. I must have fallen asleep. When I awoke it was morning. The sky was overcast, but the rain had stopped. There were only a few people still in the shuttle. I decided to go outside to see what was happening.

"The two large shuttles landed within a hundred yards of each other in a large field or pasture. Most of the passengers were gathering halfway between the two ships. There were large trees on the edges of the field but no structures to be seen anywhere. The captain and his XO were talking to each other. I couldn't hear what they were saying.

"I was cold and hungry, thinking about returning to the shuttle, when we heard a sound, like an engine, actually several engines. We couldn't tell were the sound was coming from. Then suddenly, several vehicles came flying out from behind the trees at the edge of the field and surrounded us. They had no roofs but they did have roll bars with machine guns mounted on the bars. Men stood on the backseats holding onto the guns, sweeping them back and forth across our crowd. They were all wearing similar dark green uniforms.

"We heard the sound of another vehicle, a much louder sound. After a few seconds, a motorcycle emerged and drove to the center of the circle. A very large man, also dressed in the same dark green uniform, dismounted from the motorcycle and faced our captain and XO. He shouted in a loud voice so all could hear, "Who's in charge here?"

"Our captain stepped forward extending his hand and said, 'I am.' The motorcycle driver pulled a silver handgun from a holster and shot our captain in the head. The force of the bullet lifted our captain off his feet and he flew through the air and landed on his back several feet away. 'Wrong answer.' The man placed the barrel of the gun against the XO's head and repeated his question. 'Who's in charge here?' Without hesitation, the XO said in a loud voice, 'You are, sir.' The murderer smiled at the XO and said, 'You're a smart man. Soon, trucks will come to take my new recruits to a place of training. Make sure nobody runs away or you will suffer the same fate as the man with the hole in his head.' With that he turned and mounted his motorcycle, kick started it and drove away.

"I thought to myself, *So this is what civilization has become. We're too late.*

"The trucks came, picked us up and drove us for several hours to what looked like a large military base. Men with machine guns waved us through gates in the fence that surrounded the base. For the next three months we were put through rigorous military training. Everyone, from young men and women to the quite old, were subjected to the same training for the first month and a half. They called that basic.

"We slept on the ground, got up at dawn, and were screamed at by the largest men and women I had ever seen. These people were called drill instructors, or if you were on their good side you could call them DI. We started every morning by running. First, only half a mile, but for some folks that was all they could manage. Very quickly, that was increased to a mile. By the end of basic we were running five miles every day. At the end of the second week, the men and women were separated and remained that way until all our basic training was completed. As the weeks passed, our ranks thinned noticeably. We never learned what happened to the dropouts. We never saw them again.

"It didn't matter if it rained or not, we trained. We trained in the blazing heat, we ate in the rain, we slept in the cold, but there was no giving up. We strongly suspected dropouts were eliminated.

"Basic was all about conditioning and following orders without question. Those who survived, moved on to specialized training. For two days we underwent qualification drills. If you had special skills they needed, you were grouped together with people with the same skills. You ate with them, trained with them and slept with them in barracks. No more sleeping on the ground. You also ate inside in mess halls and the food was decent.

"I survived basic and was answering questions about my skills. When I was asked what I did before becoming a soldier, I told them I was a chaplain. Nobody seemed to know what a chaplain was. I tried pastor, minister, and priest and got the same blank expression from the person doing the questioning. But when I said I had been a man of God, they understood. They began laughing hysterically. A man with officer's markings on his shoulders heard the commotion and came to investigate. When they told him I had been a man of God, he didn't laugh. Instead he grabbed me by the arm and drug me out of the building. I was sure I was to be killed immediately. Instead, I was taken to the leader, the murderer of my captain.

"The leader was busy speaking to several other officers in a large, very well appointed building. The officer who had grabbed me interrupted their discussion and whispered in the leader's ear. The discussion immediately stopped, the other officers were sent away along with the one who had brought me here.

"The leader looked me up and down like I was a piece of meat ready to be prepared for a party. Evidently, he approved of what he saw. He began to smile, an evil, wicked smile, then led me into what I assumed was his private office. It was very large, with very luxurious furnishings; a large collection of knives, swords and guns adorned the walls. He gestured towards a chair near his desk. I sat down as he moved behind the desk. He sat slowly in his chair, his eyes never leaving mine. He spoke with a deep, rumbling voice. 'So you are a man of God?'

"'I was, but no longer,' I answered.

"This interested him. He leaned forward. 'Really? Tell me why you are no longer a man of God.' I chose my words carefully. 'How can I believe in something that doesn't exist?'

"'You used to believe He existed, didn't you? What changed your mind?' He leaned forward, anxious to hear my reply.

"I thought for a moment before I replied. He was asking me questions I had never considered. 'I used to believe in a God who was merciful. One who cherished those who believed in Him. I was so sure He existed, I taught others all about Him and encouraged them to believe as I did. I came to find out that being did not exist. Or worse, he did exist, but had turned His back on us during difficult times, left us to suffer in pain and agony and ultimately to die.'

"He slammed his hand down hard on his desk and stood, towering over me. 'Yes!' he exclaimed. 'Oh yes! At last I have found someone who understands. Either there is no God or he does not care about the beings he created. Either way, he doesn't deserve our worship. Instead, put your faith in the Prince of the Air, as I have. Worship the true power on this Earth and he will make your existence a living paradise.'

"His words thrilled me to my core. I jumped up out of my seat, 'Yes, I see it clearly now. I must bring the truth to the deluded believers in a god who cares little for them. Convert them or sacrifice them on the altar of unbelief.' All the hate I felt came flowing out of me until I had no hate left and I collapsed onto the floor in my leader's office.

"When I awoke, hours had passed. I was alone. Someone had moved me to a couch. I lay there and surveyed the room. The lighting was soft and there was very relaxing music playing in the background. A door opened and the most beautiful woman I had ever seen walked toward me with a chalice in her hand. I briefly thought of my wife, but only for a moment. She had not been chosen and I was sure she had died during re-entry or before. The woman sat next to me and helped me to a sitting position. She offered me the chalice and said in a deep, sensuous voice, 'The Angel says you are one of us now, drink the elixir of life and become truly one of us in spirit as well as in body.'

"I drank deeply from the cup and the fumes effervesced through me like an electric shock. I felt reborn, with energy beyond belief. I took another deep drink and felt it even stronger. She took the cup from my hand and sat on my lap. She kissed me on the cheek, then the neck and whispered into my ear, 'Tonight I am yours. Do with me as you desire.'

"And I did.

"The next morning, I felt wonderful, unlike anything I had ever felt before. I felt no guilt whatsoever, only the determination to convert those who believed in a myth. I was given a uniform and the rank of colonel. I was made an adviser to the Angel of Death. Over the next few days, I was always by his side, learning his ways and sharing information I had about what he called the ancient's labs at New Jerusalem. I was not familiar with the name New Jerusalem, however, I assumed the ancient's lab was one of the national labs that stored equipment and supplies for the generation ships. It wasn't much, but I had knowledge of the original Jerusalem and the religious beliefs of the Jews and early Christians. He shared his knowledge about an attack that was made on the city over fifty years ago by some of his relatives.

"He told a story about how many tribes had banned together to raid the city to get the food they needed to survive. At first, they tried begging for food outside the gates, but there was no charity in the hearts of the city dwellers. When they told the guards they too believed in God and that all they were asking for was a little food, they were punished for their efforts. Finally, out of desperation, they attacked. They knew nothing about the ancient's lab under the city or all the miraculous things stored there, including weapons that could make them invincible.

"The attack went well initially, according to the oral history of the few who survived. However, they were not prepared for the level of violence the people of God rained down on them. They tried to escape, but they were pursued, hunted down like animals and slaughtered; women and children as well as the men. How could people who believed in a God of mercy be so cruel?

"So the remnants that remained turned from an uncaring God. Slowly, they rebuilt, grew, banded together, chose strong leaders with a common goal: the destruction of New Jerusalem. I became the last link in the chain that would permit their victory assault. The Angel of Death believed we were ready. Many of the crew from *Faith* had previous military training in critical disciplines to launch a war. They knew where to look for weapons, sophisticated weapons, weapons of mass destruction. More importantly, they knew how to use them.

"Once they acquired what they needed they began to march south to destroy New Jerusalem and all that it stood for."

I paused for a moment, glanced up at the the clock on the wall. I was running out of time. We had taken the truth pills just before leaving the shuttle and again at the break. They would be wearing off soon. "I'm sure you all want to know why I decided to seek asylum. About a week ago, I began having dreams, or perhaps they were visions.

"They were in two parts. In the first part, the Angel became tired of me, or feared I had betrayed him and he had decided to kill me. In the second, God was speaking to me. He showed me how he had not turned from me, but mankind had made a grave mistake thinking that they could escape the violence that would come during the end times. Mankind was meant to remain on Earth. He understood my feelings but it was now time to embrace him.

"The visions became more intense, I had written them off as pre-war jitters until a day ago. Yesterday morning, Lieutenant Cross came to me and spoke privately. He said he had a dream the Angel was going to kill me and he was supposed to take me to *Hope* and ask for asylum."

Lieutenant Cross and I were then questioned at great lengths. We gave them the answers they wanted to hear. I was beginning to worry this was taking too long

The last question concerned nuclear weapons. They wanted to know if the Angel of Death had any that he plans to use in the war? I answered, "To the best of my knowledge, he has never spoken of having nuclear weapons other than when his avatar threatened to use one against New Jerusalem. No one else in the army ever mentioned nuclear weapons." That was not the answer they were looking for, but it was the truth. I was afraid to lie at that point.

I thought we were done, but then Captain Lawrence asked me, "Have you heard anyone planning on attacking *Hope?*"

I looked at the captain and thought how best to answer. "No captain, I've never heard anyone even thinking about attacking *Hope.* However, since we've defected to your ship, I can't promise the Angel won't attack you. Even though it wouldn't be wise for him to divide his forces between two targets, don't forget, he is totally insane. No one knows for sure where his hatred will take him."

Lieutenant Cross and I were escorted from the room while they deliberated on our fate. Soon we were called back inside and told we would be given temporary asylum aboard *Hope* until the war ended. At that time there would be another vote. Also, we were to make ourselves available at anytime to answer additional questions as they arose.

The Moses and Chaplain George said they wanted to meet with me to discuss my crisis of faith. I told them I would welcome their counsel.

It was the best we could hope for.

Captain David Lawrence

The army was two days away from the gates of New Jerusalem. We had our battle plan in place. SSP Simon was responsible for the defense of New Jerusalem, XO White was responsible for the defense of *Hope,* and I was responsible for the attack on the invading army. We would strike first.

Our first move would be to beam up the armored control vehicle to a height of 300 feet and move it approximately two miles to the southwest of the city into an open field. It would be released and would free-fall into a reinforced concrete depression. It was estimated the impact velocity would be in excess of 200 miles per hour. A squad of protectors, nine men, would be in place surrounding the impact zone. Barricades would be strategically located around the drop zone to offer protection from debris caused by the impact or any detonation of explosives that may be on board the vehicle. Of course, if there was a nuke on board, everyone in the vicinity would be vaporized, but it was highly unlikely they had any nukes.

The protectors would be armed with an assortment of weapons, including laser rifles, RPGs and heavy machine guns. Their mission was to be sure the command vehicle remained entirely out of the war.

The defense of New Jerusalem focused on stopping the tanks and artillery from breaching the outer walls of the city. Fortunately, the lab contained numerous weapons that could assist in that role. It was expected the enemy would set up their artillery and begin shelling the city from several miles away. The SSP planted numerous mines in what were considered the most possible locations for the cannons to pass over.

In addition, well trained snipers were placed in hiding along the most probable routes into the city to begin harassing the troops well before they were in artillery range.

Their tanks were the biggest concern. They had massive fire power and were mobile and fast. Fortunately for us they only had five of them. The goal was to disable them before they rolled into range and began shelling the city. Special teams were assigned to each tank, armed with every weapon they could think of that might remotely have an affect on a tank, the lab could only provide a limited amount of these high power weapons.

If their troops got inside our wall, it was going to be hand-to-hand combat. Several days before the anticipated attacks, all civilians had been moved to shelters deep within the lab to wait out the battle. That included the civilians from *Hope.*

Defense of *Hope* consisted of monitoring everything in the air and establishing a perimeter completely enclosing the ship. If anything attempted to penetrate the perimeter without proper identification codes, they would be destroyed. The main defensive device for the ship was shielding used to protect it from interstellar junk when traveling at five percent of the speed of light. It's one limitation was the need to shut down shielding when the beam was used. All of *Hope's* shuttles not being used for fighting were on standby if needed to evacuate the ship.

We were ready as we could possibly be. It was time to dance.

LCDR Hiroshi Koyama

I was sitting in the Beam Room watching the movement of the attacking army as it continued to move toward New Jerusalem. *Just a little further,* I thought to myself. *Another hundred yards.*

"On my count," I whispered to the alert beam operator. " five…four…three…Two…ONE…NOW!"

The beam shot down at the speed of light and enveloped the armored command vehicle. It was a blinding white light that caused confusion; the army came to an abrupt halt. The tech engaged the tractor function, the command vehicle rose vertically off the road and continued into the sky. When it reached the needed hight to clear terrain and trees, it stopped rising. The beam and its cargo began moving laterally to southwest of the city.

The enemy troops began to panic, broke formation, running in various directions in an attempt to get away from another beam attack.

Less than a minute later, a motorcycle came screaming to the head of the column. A big man with several gold stars on his shoulders pulled a silver revolver from a holster and fired three shots into the air. Everyone froze in place. The man began shouting and the troops started forming up again. Within another minute, they were marching down the road as if nothing had happened. The big man with the gold stars and the silver revolver, holstered his gun, got on his motorcycle and roared away into the formation.

"No!" I screamed. "It's him, the leader. If only we had another beam, the war could be over before it even began."

Meanwhile, the command vehicle continued to move to the southwest. When it arrived over the field and was aligned with the concrete lined pit, the tractor function was disengaged.

The vehicle seemed to be frozen in the air for an instant, then plummeted downward building up incredible speed as it slammed into the ground. There was a tremendous explosion, thankfully not a nuclear blast, and the vehicle broke into a thousand small pieces of burning metal. No body parts were found in the wreckage.

XO Henry White

I had a bird's eye view from the captain's chair in Flight Ops. Six operators were monitoring separate regions surrounding *Hope.* One focused forward of *Hope,* one aft and one above, also called space side. The other three were focused on specific areas on the ground; one on the enemy troops as they marched towards New Jerusalem. I got an aerial view of the armored command vehicle as it was snatched from the formation and fell to its demise in a ball of fire. Another screen centered on the Temple inside the city. This one was currently looking at a long range view, which included not only the whole city, but also the surrounding farm land and rural homes. Residents of those homes had been evacuated several days ago and the home owners now sheltered in facilities deep within the ancient's lab. The last screen was now tracking the movements of the five enemy tanks. They broke off from the troops and appeared to be moving to encircle the city walls.

The operators of each screen had a point of contact on the ground through encrypted channels that enabled them to intercept the enemy and eliminate their ability to attack. As a famous general once said, "We're going to find them and kill them before they get the chance to start killing us."

The lead tank was making very good speed across rolling terrain. They were coming up on a small stream they would have to cross if they wanted to get in position on the far side of the city, away from the main gate. They appeared to be following a well used trail that forded the stream at its shallowest location. It barely reduced its speed before nosing slightly down into the stream.

At that point the entire front end of the tank exploded as the six mines located just under the surface of the water were detonated by the impact of the tank. The explosions were so intense they lifted the entire turret off the body of the tank, hurling it spinning into the air. Before it came crashing down, four protectors in watertight gear popped up out of the water, each with an RPG launcher, and fired a round into the tank's treads. The tank was now dead in the water as the turret came crashing down. One down, four to go.

The screen showing tactical movements now picked up the artillery being deployed. The range of the cannons varied, however they were not mobile like the cannons on the tanks. The rule of thumb for artillery was to be as far away from your target as possible. That was your only defense. Except in this case, several of the protectors from New Jerusalem set up shop in three abandoned homes on the outskirts of the farmland. They had a direct line of sight to the cannons and were well within range with their very sophisticated mortar launchers. Under the cover of darkness they had brought in over a hundred rounds of mortar shells for each site. In addition to the mortar operators, each farm house had a squad of riflemen to provide covering fire.

They waited until the enemy troops had marched away from the artillery. Then they opened up with a withering barrage of mortar fire on each of the artillery batteries. Within minutes, there wasn't a functioning artillery piece left.

I smiled to myself and thought, *this is going to be so easy. These men may be well trained, but they aren't seasoned warriors. This might be over in time for me to get a workout in before dinner.*

Then we lost all power to the ship, the warning klaxons were screaming throughout *Hope.* I said a short prayer for our observer in the aft shuttle bay.

Lieutenant Cross

When the lights went out I quickly removed my right boot, turned the heal and reached inside the secret compartment and took out the package and a small knife. The chaplain was still sitting besides me as the previously locked door swung open. When he began to standup, I said, "Don't move yet. I quickly grabbed the chaplain and said, "Help me up."

I grabbed him around the waste and made a quick three inch cut between his ribs. He bagan to scream in pain as I shove the package between his exposed ribs and into his body.

"What's the matter?" I yelled. "Are you okay? Are you hurt?"

"What did you do to me?" he screamed.

"I didn't do anything. Oh my God, you're bleeding. You need to get to a doctor. I have to go meet the Angel. Go find the doctor. The med bay is just down the hall to your right." I helped him out into the hall and pushed him away from the med bay. I turned and began moving to the aft shuttle bay.

Captain David Lawrence

I was on the bridge when the power went out. It seemed like it took a lifetime for the emergency power to kick in. It turned out it was longer than a lifetime for some of my crew. Fifteen minutes later, the emergency power system also failed. We were totally blind, except for the small lights in our personal com units.

I commed Hiroshi. "Where are you?"

"I'm on my way to the aft shuttle bay. Looks like you we're right, cap. I should be there in ten minutes."

"Roger that. Actually, it was Simon who got it right. Com me when you arrive," I said, then commed Henry. "Have you made it to the holding area yet?" I asked the XO.

"Just arrived, cap. The doors are wide open and nobody's home."

"With the power off, all the doors unlock. I think they were counting on that. Head to the aft shuttle bay. Hiroshi and I will meet you there. Do you think you can find it in the dark?"

"How can you ask me that, cap?" asked the XO. "You know I do my best work in the dark."

The three of us met up at the hatch leading into the shuttle bay. "Have they left yet?" asked the XO.

"Pretty sure they have," I answered. "I want to make sure before we turn the power back on."

We quick-walked across the shuttle bay floor to the parking location of their shuttle. It was empty. I commed the bridge, "This is Captain Lawrence, restart all power generators." Within minutes, *Hope* was back to full power.

While we waited I asked Henry, "You contacted SSP Simon to expect visitors, didn't you?"

"Was I supposed to do that?" he said with a look of feigned terror in his eyes. "Oh cap, I'm so sorry, I thought Hiroshi was supposed … Of course I contacted him. A man doesn't get to be the XO if he can't follow simple orders."

"Just checking," I laughed, then added, "Even captain's forget things once in a while."

Hiroshi spoke up, "Like when you forgot the final toast at my wedding?"

I ignored him and said, "I think we have a war to fight, gentlemen. Let's get to it."

SSP Simon

We waited in silence for the shuttle. The Moses refused to leave the Temple and was now with us just inside the opened doors to the balcony. It was beginning to get dark and the sound of the war was rolling across the farmlands right to us. The battle was going in our favor, that didn't mean we didn't have losses. Besides the sounds of guns and cannons firing were the cries and screams of the wounded and the dying.

We didn't have to wait long. The shuttle circled overhead and sat down silently in the plaza beneath the balcony. Two people got out and walked toward the Temple's main entrance. They disappeared as they passed under the balcony, but we could clearly hear the sound of two large Temple doors opening and then closing. The way to the main sanctuary was lit by torches on either side of the hall. A deep voice invited them to enter. "Good evening, Pilgrims. Please take a seat. The Moses will be with you soon. Please use this time to meditate on your lives and all of the blessings our God has bestowed on you."

I and six well armed protectors took a silent elevator down to the first level and stepped into the dark shadows near the wall. Their weapons were at the ready.

A light shown down from the high dome over the altar illuminating the Moses, dressed in his finest robes, as if he were prepared to hold a worship service. "Good evening, gentlemen. Only two of you tonight? I thought there would be one more. Where is Chaplain Dekker?"

One of the men stood and said, "The chaplain was unavoidably detained. I'm Lieutenant Cross, personal pilot for my Lord and

Master, The Angel of Death. He has come to accept your surrender."

"Has he now? And why would he think we would consider surrendering?"

The Angel of Death slowly stood and addressed the Moses, "Why, to prevent the annihilation of all your people, of course."

"I believe it is your people who are being annihilated, not ours. Our victory is close to certainty. Perhaps I should be accepting your surrender."

"Ah," he said, "you are referring to the battle being waged outside your city walls. That's merely a diversion. The outcome is of no concern to me."

"Really, you know, I've heard it said that you are a worshiper of the Prince of the Air. He is also known as the Father of Liars. Perhaps you are indulging in one of your own fabrications."

"If you believe your God will save you and your city, you are the one deluding yourself. Ask Chaplain Dekker how your God saved the people of *Faith*. Better yet, ask him how your God turned his back on him and let five thousand people die in vain, gnawing the flesh from their own bones in a futile attempt to survive? No, your God will not save you. On the other hand, my God has given me the power to remove you and your followers from this place forever and all those on the generation ship *Hope* as well. There will be no *Hope* at all for them when I am finished."

"Well, if you, with the help of your God, Satan, are going to annihilate us, why bother to ask us to surrender? Slaughter us and be done with it. Personally, I'm bored with your boasting." The Moses turned and began to walk away.

"Wait," he yelled angrily, but also with a touch of panic. He turned and pointed to the courtyard and said, "The shuttle that sits outside your precious Temple contains a one megaton nuclear bomb. When I detonate it all of New Jerusalem and the precious ancient's lab will be vaporized in the blink of an eye."

The Moses stopped, turned back to look at him, and began laughing. "Liar!" he shouted. "Just like your father, you are a liar. And a poor liar at that. Apparently you believe if you tell a lie often enough, people will believe you. You poor, pathetic little man." He turned abruptly and really walked away this time.

The man screamed at the Moses. "Don't you turn your back on me. Don't you dare turn your back on me!" As he said it, he reached for his silver revolver, pulled back the hammer and died instantly from a barrage of bullets from the protector's weapons. The pilot was also killed.

The lights in the sanctuary glowed brighter and two protectors began to clear the bodies away. The avatar of the Moses standing on the stage blinked out and the real Moses stepped out of the shadows shaking his head. "He truly was insane."

Another protector came running into the sanctuary screaming. "I think there's a bomb in the shuttle! I saw a blinking red light through the window. It's a timer counting down."

Doctor Soo Song

I was alone in my med bay, double checking our preparation to receive injured warriors. Everything seemed to be in order when the lights went out. I heard the klaxons begin to scream out their warning as I stood there in the dark. A few seconds later, the lights returned as the backup generators kicked in.

I was surprised to see a man standing at the med bay entrance. He was obviously in distress, he looked dazed and confused. As I moved to assist him, I noticed his eyes; one blue and one brown. He was the chaplain from *Faith.*

He tried to step toward me, but stumbled. I was able to reach him in time to keep him from falling to the floor. He resisted my help at first He stepped back and tried to push my hands away. He was so disoriented and weak I fnally managed to get him on to a nearby gurney. As I strapped him in and began to connect monitor leads, he began to shake; he was having a grand mal seizure. His eyes rolled back into his head and white foam was drooling from his mouth. I reached for an injection gun and dialed in a setting. I placed the gun against his neck and pulled the trigger, within a few minutes his shaking subsided and his eyes began to focus. He lips were moving as he tried to speak. At first I couldn't make out what he was trying to say.

He paused for an instant to catch his breath. He turned his head and stared at me, there was fear in his expression as he said, "I'm a bomb!"

LCRD Hiroshi Koyama

I had just returned to the Beam Room when an emergency call came in from SSP Simon. There was a lot of talking and yelling in the background and I didn't catch what he said at first. I could hear him yell for everyone to shut up and it quickly became silent.

"Hiroshi, there is a small shuttle in the Temple plaza. We think there's a bomb inside, a nuclear bomb. I pray to God you can help us. We can't get in and the timer is counting down."

"On it," I said. I gave the location to the beam tech and he quickly located the target and locked on with maximum lift. Simon gave me a running description of what was happening.

"I see the beam … the shuttle just lifted off from the plaza … it's moving upward at a high rate of speed … I can no longer see it, can you beam it into space? We need to get to shelter. We have no idea about the strength of the bomb, praise God you were able to help …"

His com cut off as a brilliant flash lit up the sky. A few seconds later *Hope* was blasted with a tremendous shockwave that knocked me to the deck.

Once again, the ship went dark as the klaxons began blaring their warning.

Doctor Soo Song

The med bay went dark again, Fortunatley I was able to get to my control center. I pushed the button for battery power and the light returned. It was such a relief, the med bay had its own independent backup system and I could hear the lights hum as they kicked in.

I returned to check on my patient and looked at his vitals; his temperature had risen two degrees in the short time he had been in med bay. His face was now very flushed and I notice blistering on his neck, I removed his shirt and saw more blistering and the wound from a recent surgery, very recent. I quickly grabbed a radiation meter and scanned his body, he was off the charts. I donned a radiation suit and commed Hiroshi as I did a full body MRI.

"Hiroshi, Chaplain Dekker is in med bay with a nuclear bomb in his body. He is dangerously radioactive. We need to get him off the ship as soon as possible."

"Another nuke?!!" Hiroshi exclaimed, he was in the med bay within minutes. "The beam is off line. We're going to have to eject him off the ship and pray he's far enough away when the bomb goes off," he said as he put on his own radiation suit.

While Hiroshi finished suiting up, I prepared an injection for the chaplain. It would take away his pain and put him into a coma that would last several hours … or until the bomb detonated. As I placed the injection gun next to his neck, his eyes fluttered open. The white of his eyes were now completely red. He asked me, "Are you an angel?"

I answered truthfully, "No, I'm here to take away your pain."

He smiled briefly as I pushed the button on the injection gun. His last words were, "May God bless you for your merciful ways."

Hiroshi and I guided the power gurney down the hallway to the launch bay, adjacent to the shuttle bay at the aft end of the ship. I could feel the ship shuddering as we ran. The ship-wide emergency lights came back on just as we passed through the hatch. I prayed we could get the chaplain off the ship in time.

We lifted him off of the gurney into a launch tube. Launch tubes were usually used for ejecting garbage that couldn't be recycled. It seemed like the proper way to dispose of a traitor. I said another prayer, this time a prayer of praise for the launch system being pneumatic; our electric power was still out. Hiroshi manually launched the tube with a loud *whooshing* sound and he was gone.

I looked at my wrist chrono and wondered how far away he had to be before we were out of danger. We stood there waiting as we tried to catch our breaths from the long sprint to the launch bay. After two minutes, I began to relax.

Too soon.

A few seconds later the bomb went off.

There were no windows in the launch bay, so we couldn't see the flash of the explosion. There is no atmosphere in space to transmit sound. The way we knew he had exploded was the way the ship lurched and bucked. Since there was an atmosphere inside the launch bay, we could easily hear the shriek of metal being torn apart, followed by the hissing sound of the atmosphere as it leaked from the ship into space!

And of course, the lights went out, plunging us into total darkness once again.

LCDR Hiroshi Koyama

There was barely enough light from our coms for Dr. Song and me to make our way out of the launch bay. The hatch bulkhead seemed intact enough We were able to close and seal the hatch behind us. Unfortunately, we could both hear air leaking out of other areas in the aft part of our ship. We were able to make it back to the med bay, sealing all the hatches as we went after making sure no one was trapped in any of the aft compartments.

Injured crew members were waiting in the med bay when we arrived and several of her assistant's reported to duty; they were busy triaging the injured. I left Dr. Song to deal with the wounded and made my way back to the bridge to give my damage report to the captain and fill him in on the bombings.

211

It took me a long time to make it to the bridge. Several passageways were collapsed and others were clogged with debris. I lost count of the number of times I had to backtrack and start over. When I was half way there, power was restored, and, one by one, systems were coming back online. When I finally made it to the bridge, things were in shambles. The captain was trying to talk to the Moses, but the com system was erratic. The XO was completely absorbed in fighting the war. Apparently, four of the tanks had been destroyed, but one made it through the blockade and was beginning to shell the city. So far, the Temple remained unscathed. The mortar team that had destroyed the artillery was being moved into position to attack the last tank.

On the positive side, many enemy troops were surrendering in mass. There were many reports of enemy officers being fragged by their own troops, followed by the immediate surrendering of those involved. I got most of this by eavesdropping on various bridge conversations. Everyone was so involved with their piece of the war.

I spotted the captain, just in time to see him throw his com against the nearest bulkhead. He used some salty Navy language to demonstrate his displeasure with the device. He noticed me standing there with my mouth opened and he motioned me to join him, pointing in the direction of his ready room.

Once inside, he said, "We have to evacuate the ship. It's been damaged beyond repair. I've been trying to speak with the Moses about providing temporary accommodation for all of us, but the blasted com systems aren't working. I need you to go down and talk to him in person to plead our case. They are already taking care of over four thousand of our people in the ancient's lab. I'm hoping they can handle the rest of us."

212

There was a sudden burst of cheering from the bridge and the XO stuck his head into the ready room and yelled, "The mortar team destroyed the last tank and the army has been routed, they're on the run. The war is over!" He closed the door leaving the two of us alone.

I quickly briefed the captain on the two nuclear bombs and how they were handled. He just shook his head. "What a waste. What a needless waste."

I could tell he was close to tears, but he put his own feelings aside and said to me, "The beam is operational again. Beam down to the Temple and speak with the Moses or the SSP. See if you can get them to agree to the rest of the crew coming down. Tell them the truth; the two nuclear explosions have damaged *Hope* beyond repair. We are going to have to abandon her and then scuttle her. We can't leave her in orbit. If we do it's only a matter of time before the orbit decays and she re-enters. She's too big to burn up during re-entry and she could kill thousands of people if she comes down in a populated area."

He paused for a moment to gather his thoughts. "Tell them the XO and I are working on a plan to scuttle her." He paused again then said, "Before you return, please visit the civilians and tell them the fighting is over and we'll all be united soon. Spend some time with Anna before you return and say hello to Miriam. Tell her I miss her, miss her very much. Tell her I will be with her as soon as I can." He paused again and I could see he was struggling to maintain his composure.

He said abruptly, "Now get the hell out of here," and turned his back to me. I left quickly.

The Moses

Thank God, the war is over and New Jerusalem is intact. But look at the price that was paid. So many people died. What a tragedy. The smell of blood hangs heavy in the air. How do we move forward? There are so many changes coming. How do we decide which path to follow?

For the first time in my life, I feel overwhelmed. It was all so simple when we followed the old traditions. We never doubted we were on the right path, the path that God had directed us to follow. Then the stranger came, and our world will never be the same. We thought we knew the truth, it turned out our truth was a partial truth, an incomplete truth. I'm sad to say I was willing; no, not willing, *eager* to kill the stranger to preserve our incomplete truth. However, he escaped my hatred and, instead of seeking vengeance for my death sentence, showed me a better way, a complete truth. Now as the leader of my people, I must share the complete truth with them all. The stranger and his friends risked their lives to preserve ours. Why would they do that? They were willing to risk their very existence, their way of life, to ensure that we, total strangers, would survive. What type of people would do that? That is the question. The answer is: Those who know the complete truth.

When you know the complete truth, know it so deeply it becomes a part of you, you don't need ten thousand written laws to govern your life because the important law is written on your heart. The Messiah said it and it applies to all mankind: Love one another as I have loved you.

SSP Simon

I was busy ensuring the enemy prisoners were being rounded up. I was overwhelmed by the number who had surrendered instead of trying to escape. It seemed they never wanted to go to war in the first place. They were forced into service by that madman and his henchmen. Most of them never even fired their weapons. One man told me the only person he shot was his leader.

I saw Hiroshi beam down and rushed to thank him for saving the Tempe and probably all of New Jerusalem from the nuclear bomb. When he told me what it did to *Hope,* I was in shock.

When he told me about the second bomb placed inside of the chaplain and how it exploded very close to the ship, I was totally stunned. I didn't know what to say. Then he said the two explosions damaged *Hope* so badly they would have to abandon her. I was almost in tears. I cried out to him, "What can we do to help you? I had no idea all this occurred. Did you lose many crew members? Did the captain survive? The XO?"

He told me they had very few fatalities, however many were injured. They would have to abandon ship as soon as possible; it was beginning to come apart. They needed a place to stay. "With us," I said without thinking. "You will all stay with us in New Jerusalem. We owe you our very existence."

He thanked me profusely, then went to meet with his wife and *Hope's* civilians sequestered in the ancient's lab. I left to find the Moses to relay all the information Hiroshi just told me.

Anna

I was so worried. We had been told the war was over and that we had won, but nobody could tell us about *Hope*. Someone heard about two nuclear bombs exploding in space. The Temple wasn't damaged at all due to the actions of the crew of *Hope,* again, they had no information about *Hope*.

Miriam was standing with me when we heard about the nuclear bombs. I had no idea what that really meant. To me a bomb was a bomb, but when Miriam heard the word 'nuclear' her knees buckled and she gave a short scream and began crying. I held her to try to comfort her, but when she told me how much worse a nuclear bomb was, I joined her with my own tears. She said the two big earthquakes we felt weren't earthquakes at all. They were the shockwaves caused by nuclear explosions; felt even though they had gone off so far away in space.

Hope's civilians had been moved to the temporary facilities set up in the ancient's lab almost a week before the fighting began. Fear gripped our hearts from then on. We got very little information since arriving. We were both worried sick, we couldn't eat, hardly slept at all, we weren't alone; there was a large contingency of families who's loved ones were still on *Hope*.

Everyone was exhausted. We tried to sleep, but dreams and nightmares made it impossible to get any rest. One afternoon, I lay dozing on my cot. I was having a recurring dream of sorts. I could hear Hiroshi's voice calling me. I would call back, but he would never hear me. His voice would become fainter and fainter until it faded away completely.

This time the dream was different. His voice kept getting louder, then I heard Miriam say, "Hiroshi? Hiroshi is that you?"

Then someone was shaking me. It was the most lifelike dream I ever had. I didn't want to wake up. I wanted to cherish this moment forever. I wanted to live in this dream until it was real. Miriam kept shaking me until I nearly fell off my cot. "Wake up girl. He's really here!"

My eyes fluttered open, and there he was. The most beautiful man I'd ever seen. "It's about time," I screamed, as I leaped from the cot into his waiting arms. It was really him, I could tell by his beard scratching my face, and by his man-smell. This was definitely my Hiroshi.

He couldn't stop kissing me nor I him. I was hugging him so tightly, I got a cramp in my arm and had to let go. As I did, I noticed all the people gathered around us hoping to hear about their own loved ones. Miriam was pulling on his arm now. "What about my Dave, is my captain all right? Please tell me he's all right," she said as tears streaked down her face.

Hiroshi turned to her and took her hand as he said, "Your husband is fine, Miriam. He asked me to tell you he loves you dearly and will see you as soon as he can." Her look of fear melted away at the news, and she collapsed onto her cot and began crying even harder. This time they were tears of joy.

Everyone was asking questions about the fate of their loved ones. Hiroshi stepped up on my cot and yelled, "Listen up, everyone, quiet please. Let me tell you what I know." The crowd quickly became quite and inched closer to Hiroshi.

"First of all, the war is over. Casualties in New Jerusalem are light, very light. Casualties on *Hope* are even lighter." There was brief cheering, Hiroshi waved for silence and continued. "There were two nuclear explosions close to *Hope* and she was severely damaged. We are going to have to evacuate the ship as soon as possible. Most of the crew will begin evacuation immediately, but a skeleton crew will remain to scuttle the ship."

Someone shouted, "Where will we live?"

"We will be relocating into New Jerusalem, but that will take some time. Initially, we'll remain in the ancient's lab, however all families will be reunited. I can guarantee you that."

He turned to me with a sad smile and I knew what that meant. "I'm so sorry. I have to go," he said. "I'll come back to see you as often as I can. In the meantime, please help Miriam coordinate things here. You've lived in New Jerusalem for several years. Tell them the good things about the city. I promise you, things will change for the better."

I kissed him goodbye. I was a little sad to see him go, but at the same time I was so relieved that he was all right. I felt optimistic. New Jerusalem was not such a bad place to live, as long as the protectors left you alone. I believed my husband; things would change for the better.

XO Henry White

The evacuation of *Hope* was complete. It took several days of shuttle trips to get everyone down to New Jerusalem along with a limited amount of their personal gear. We took all the livestock from the farmland as well. Following the evacuation, we stripped the ship of everything we thought we could use on the surface. All of Dr. Song's med bay was disassembled and shuttled down along with all her medication supplies. The Beam Room equipment also went, as well as electronic equipment from Flight Ops and the Bridge. The propulsion system was not salvageable nor was anything else from the aft end of the ship. It was pretty much radioactive slag. Radiation barriers were installed to keep from contaminating the rest of the ship.

They left me with just enough equipment to nudge *Hope* out of its orbit and send it on its way to the sun. It was the only safe option we had. Hiroshi and a few other crew members were on board. The last shuttle, a medium sized class, was in the forward shuttle bay, waiting to get us down to the landing zone just outside New Jerusalem's outer wall. It was close to where new houses were being constructed for our crew and their families. I had managed to sneak about a ton of weights and equipment aboard the shuttle. It was a perk cap allowed me for handling the scuttling of *Hope*. So many dreams were tied to this ship. I wondered what happened to those that set up the colony on Proxima B. We'd probably never know in our lifetimes, that would be for future generations to know.

It was time to go. We fired the maneuvering rockets to break orbit and made sure the heading was correct. After that, there was nothing to do. The gravity of our sun would pull *Hope* into her fiery grave.

We headed for the forward shuttle bay. I had removed the ship's plaque and collected all the pictures of *Hope's* officers over the 200 years. They were all stored safely aboard. We had plans to build a museum dedicated to the memory of *Hope* and her generations of crews. We faced the ship's flag hanging above the bay door and came to attention and saluted the flag. We held the salute as Taps played over the PA system. When it ended we snapped our hands down and Hiroshi did a crisp left-face and said to me, "Permission to leave the ship, sir?"

I said in return, "Permission granted, Lieutenant Commander."

I turned to the bosun and said, "Bosun, Pipe us off the ship for the last time."

The young man put the pipe to his lips and blew the high pitched, three note refrain. It seemed to echo over and over in the empty bay. When I could hear it no longer I said, "Gentlemen, abandon ship."

We marched to the shuttle and boarded her. The pilot maneuvered her through the open bay door and headed to the surface and our new home.

We never looked back.

The End

About the Author

Frank G. Davis

Frank is a long time resident of Arizona. He moved from Oregon in 1965 to attend graduate school at Arizona State University. After earning his Master of Science degree in Engineering, he began his professional career as an engineer at a local aerospace company designing gas turbine engines. After 22 years as an engineer, he received an MBA and became a sales manager for the Allied-Signal Corporation. This new position provided the opportunity to travel extensively to numerous Asian and European countries. He retired in 2001 after 36 years of service.

During those 36 years he also became a commercial pilot and flight instructor, a power lifter, and earned black belts in three different styles of martial arts. He continues to train and has reached the level of San Dan in Shotokan Karate. He was also an Assistant Professor at the College of Engineering at ASU for a year.

Since retirement he and his wife of 45 years, Alicia, have become very active in their church. Recently, he began to return to writing, mostly science fiction, a hobby that he dabbled in off and on for most of his life. Several things happened that led to this novel: a series of inspirational sermons, ideas for stories that "popped into his head," and the corona virus pandemic which restricted him to his house. He figured he might as well get serious about writing.

Enjoy all the works of Frank G. Davis
Available in both paperback and ebook

Future Histories

Four short stories from the future

1. Real
2. The Elect
3. Zombie Pilgrims
4. Stephen

Professor Radcliff's Time Machine

A university professor takes his students on a
wild ride through time from an ancient Pharaoh
to the end of the world.

The first two books of the Generations
Trilogy

Join the crew of the generation ship *Hope* as
they return from Alpha Centauri to find the
world decimated by a plague. See how they join
with Earth's survivors to build a new
civilization. The last book of the trilogy will
be released in February, 2021.

For more information on these books, go to:

scififrank.com